Princess
of the
Midnight
Ball

Princess
of the
Midnight
Ball

Jessica Day George

BLOOMSBURY

New York · Berlin · London

280

Published by Bloomsbury U.S.A. Children's Books
175 Fifth Avenue, New York, New York 10010

Library of Congress Cataloging-in-Publication Data
George, Jessica Day.
Princess of the Midnight Ball / by Jessica Day George. — 1st U.S. ed.
p.   cm.
Summary: A retelling of the tale of twelve princesses who wear out their
shoes dancing every night, and of Galen, a former soldier now working
in the king's gardens, who follows them in hopes of breaking the curse.
ISBN-13: 978-1-59990-322-4 • ISBN-10: 1-59990-322-9
[1. Fairy tales. 2. Princesses—Fiction. 3. Dancing—Fiction. 4. Soldiers—Fiction.
5. Magic—Fiction. 6. Blessing and cursing—Fiction.] I. Title.
PZ8.G3295Pri 2009   [Fic]—dc22   2008030310

First U.S. Edition 2009
Book design by Donna Mark
Typeset by Westchester Book Composition
Printed in the U.S.A. by Quebecor World Fairfield
2 4 6 8 10 9 7 5 3 1

All papers used by Bloomsbury U.S.A. are natural, recyclable products
made from wood grown in well-managed forests. The manufacturing processes
conform to the environmental regulations of the country of origin.

For Jenn
Finally

Princess
of the
Midnight
Ball

Prologue

Because he had once been human, the King Under Stone sometimes found himself plagued by human emotions. He was experiencing one now, as he faced the mortal woman before him, but it took a moment for him to give it a name. After a pause he labeled it "triumph."

"Do you understand our bargain?" The king had a voice like a steel blade breaking on stone.

"I do." The human queen's voice was steady. "Twelve years will I dance for you here below, and in return Westfalin shall be victorious."

"Let us not forget the years you still owe me," the king said. "Our first bargain is not yet fulfilled."

"I know." She bowed her head in weariness. There were dark circles beneath her eyes and gray in her hair though she was a young woman still.

The King Under Stone stretched out his long white hand and lifted her chin. "What a pity your daughters do not join you at our little fetes," he said. "Such lovely girls, I am sure. And my twelve sons are pining for companionship." Again the feeling of triumph: the idea of these mortal girls dancing with his sons. There had always been the little problem, as his sons grew older, of where to find them brides.

Beautiful brides who could walk in the sun.

And then this mortal queen had come to *him*, begging for aid in bearing children with her fat, foolish husband. She had borne seven daughters so far, and once she had borne a dozen, Under Stone had decided that he would find a way to bring the girls below to meet their future husbands.

A look of horror spread across the queen's face at his suggestion. "My d-daughters are s-sweet, honorable girls," she stuttered. "And young. Too young to be married!"

"Ah, but my sons are young, and their dear mothers were all sweet, honorable women, just like yourself and your little daughters! And my princes do long for companions of their own kind." Each of Under Stone's sons had been born to a mortal woman, and he wanted their wives to be mortal as well. The King Under Stone brushed back a stray curl of the queen's hair.

She drew back. "Are we finished? I must go... the children... my husband...."

"Yes, yes." He waved a long hand. "Our bargain is made. You may go."

She turned and hurried away. Away from the black palace on the shadowy shore. A silent figure, cloaked and hooded, rowed her across the sunless lake in a silver filigree boat and escorted her to the gate that led to the sunlight world.

The King Under Stone smiled as he watched Queen Maude hurry away. She would be back. She had to come back, every week. But that was not what made him smile. She had concealed her condition for quite some time, but as she settled into the boat it became apparent that the human queen was expecting her eighth child, precisely on schedule.

"Another precious little princess for her and her darling Gregor," Under Stone said, the cold semblance of human feeling just barely tingeing his voice. "And another beautiful bride for one of my sons."

Soldier

Exhausted almost beyond the point of thought, Galen never-theless kept moving forward, alone in the middle of the dusty road. In his head he sang the marching song of his old regi-ment, but his feet stumbled more than they marched.

Left, left, left, left, left my wife and children too! Did I do right, right, right, right, right?

He laughed a little to himself. He was not quite nineteen years old, and he had spent most of his life on the battlefield. He had no wife or children to leave, only filthy tents, bad food, and death. Before him lay the endless road, dust, thirst, and life. Or so he hoped.

He drank the last swig of water from his canteen, hung it back on his belt, and stumbled on. The wind bit through his worn soldier's coat; winter was coming.

All around him were fields that had lain fallow for years. In one, turnips that some hopeful family had planted had rot-ted in the earth with no one to harvest them. In another, the weeds were as tall as Galen. A cow and her calf were feasting there, and Galen veered from his path, taking a step toward them. They looked abandoned, so no one would mind if he filled his canteen with milk. But when he took a second step in their direction, the cow lowed with alarm and trotted away, her calf at her heels. She had been running wild for too long to suffer being milked.

With a sigh, Galen continued on. Every so often he came across other soldiers heading home. He would share a meager meal and camp with them overnight, walking for a while the next morning in the familiar company of other exhausted fighting men in blue tunics. But Galen never stayed with these other soldiers for long, something that they found very odd. It was said that in the heat of battle strangers became brothers and the bond was not severed by death or distance. Galen had never felt that way, though. He had seen his first battle when he was seven years old, had helped his mother care for the wounded and watched her wash enemy blood out of his father's uniform afterward. To Galen, war was a disease, something to be avoided, not something he wanted to talk about with other afflicted men over the campfire.

Sometimes women or men too old to join the fight would offer him a ride in their cart. They often wanted to know if he had met their son or husband during the war. It was rare that he had: the army was vast, and Galen's regiment had been from the city of Isen, far from these fields and forests.

Galen told people what he could, making light of the conditions the soldiers had lived in and celebrating with them

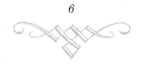

over the end of the war. Westfalin had defeated the Analousians at last, but it was a grim victory. After twelve years at war, the country was deeply in debt to her allies, and many soldiers would not be returning home. Or, like Galen, they no longer had a home to return to.

The son of a soldier and an army laundress, Galen had been born in a cottage that looked out on the training grounds where his father marched in drills all day long. When he was six, the Analousians had attacked, and Galen's father's regiment had been sent to the front lines. His mother, the daughter of a soldier herself, had packed up Galen and his baby sister and joined the supply train. She had scrubbed blue tunics and darned gray socks right up until the day the lung sickness— a gift of the damp and cold—had claimed her life. Galen's little sister, Ilsa, had also suffered from lung sickness. She had recovered, but her breath often came short, and so she had ridden on the supply wagons during the marches. She was killed when the wagon she was riding slipped off a steep mountain road in the rain and fell into the river below.

By that time Galen was twelve. He had been working with the soldiers since his eighth birthday: fetching powder and shot, reloading rifles and pistols, carrying messages from the generals to the field marshals. He could shoot a rifle or pistol, use a bayonet, peel potatoes, splint a broken leg, shine boots, wash shirts, and knit his own socks. He could also spit six feet with great accuracy, swear like the best of the sergeants, and scream insults at the Analousians in their own tongue. His father had been very proud.

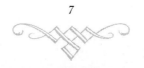

Galen's father made sergeant, and then lost his life to an Analousian bullet one morning when Galen was fifteen. Galen had buried him in the common grave dug after that battle, shouldered his father's weapons, and marched away to the next skirmish. He didn't know it, but just a week later, he shot the man who had killed his father, putting a bullet neatly into the same place his father had been shot—an inch to the left of the heart.

Those days were past, God be praised, and Galen hoped to never kill another man. He was headed north and east, away from Analousia and toward the heart of Westfalin. He hoped to find his mother's family in the capital city of Bruch. With so many men lost in battle, Galen prayed that there might be a place for him at his aunt's house, and in the family business as well. He couldn't quite remember what his mother had said it was, but he thought that his uncle did something with trees. It seemed strange that he would find much work as a wood-cutter in the heart of the city, but Galen wasn't picky. He needed work, and food, and a place to rest his weary bones.

"Oh, my weary, weary bones!"

Galen stopped trudging with a start as someone echoed his thought. On the side of the road, a bundle of rags rearranged itself into a very old woman in a tattered dress and shawl. She stared up at Galen with bright blue eyes, her back bent and humped.

"Hello there, young soldier!"

"Hello there, goodfrau," he replied.

"I don't suppose you have anything for an old woman to eat?" She smacked her lips, revealing very few teeth.

With a groan Galen took off his pack and laid it on the ground. He groaned even louder as he lowered himself to sit next to the old woman. "Let's see, shall we?"

He didn't feel, as some other soldiers did, that the rest of the country owed him something. They had fought a war, true, but it was their job. The civilians had continued their jobs as well. Seamstresses had sewed, blacksmiths shod horses and made nails, those farmers not pressed into service had continued to farm. And Galen's parents had instilled in him a deep respect for women and his elders, and the ancient creature before him was both.

He rummaged in his pack. "I've drunk the last of my water, but I do have a swallow of wine here in this skin," he said, laying it before them. "I have three hard biscuits, a wedge of old cheese, and a packet of dried meat. I also have some late berries I picked this morning." He felt a pang at offering these up: he had been saving them as a special treat. But he would feel even worse if he denied this old woman something that might give her pleasure as well.

"Not enough teeth for the dried meat, or the biscuits," she said, grinning to reveal even more gaps than Galen had noticed before. "But I wouldn't mind a little cheese and wine, just like the fancy folks in the palace feast on."

Galen had two of the hard biscuits, and wished afterward that he had not. He had no water, and the old woman

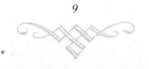

swallowed the wine in one gulp. Then she ate the cheese with much eye rolling and lip smacking, until he found himself smiling at her gusto.

Arching one eyebrow, the crone looked at the berries. "Care to share, dearie?"

"Of course." Galen pushed them closer to her. She took a handful and slipped them into her mouth one at a time, savoring them as she had the cheese and wine. Glad that she had not taken the entire bag for herself, Galen scooped up his portion and ate them with equal pleasure.

"Returning from the war, are you?" Now that her hunger was sated, the old woman looked Galen over.

"Yes, goodfrau," he said shortly. He didn't want to know the name of the grandson, or great-grandson, who had been lost to an Analousian bullet.

He rewrapped the remaining biscuit, folded the cheese cloth and the berry bag, and stowed everything neatly in his pack. He put the wineskin on top, hoping to beg a swallow or two at the next farmhouse. "I was on the front lines." Galen wasn't sure why he added this, but it was his one source of pride. He had been to the front lines, and he had survived.

"Ah." The crone shook her head sadly. "A bad business, that. Worse than it needed to be, you know." She laid a finger alongside her crooked nose, winking.

Galen shook his head. "I don't understand."

She just sucked her teeth and nodded wisely. "Just you remember: when you make a deal with them as lives below, there's always a hidden price." She nodded again.

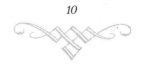

"I see," Galen said in confusion. "Thank you." He didn't see. In fact, he thought the crone was quite senile, but it was hardly any of his concern. "I'd best keep on while there's still daylight," he said, standing up and shouldering his pack.

"Indeed, indeed, for the nights are cold," the old woman said, clambering to her feet as well. She shivered and wrapped her thin shawl about her shoulders. "The days are cold, too."

Galen didn't hesitate. He unwrapped one of the scarves around his neck and offered it to her. It was blue wool, and very warm. "Here, granny, take this."

"I could not deprive you, poor soldier," she said even as she reached for it.

"I've another," he said kindly. "Plus wool and needles, should I wish to make more."

Holding the scarf up to the weak sunlight, the crone admired the tight knitting. "Make this yourself, did you?"

"Aye. There's time enough between battles to knit a dozen scarves and a hundred stockings, as well I know." He gave a little bark of laughter.

"I thought soldiers spent their idle time dicing and wenching." She gave a surprisingly girlish giggle.

"Dicing and wenching is all very well, but it doesn't do you much good when there are holes in your socks and snow falling through the holes in your tent," he said grimly. Then he shook off the memory. "Wear it in good health."

Galen wished that he had a shawl to give her, for the one she wore had great snags in it. But the only shawl he had ever knit had been given to a general's daughter with soft brown eyes.

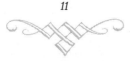

"You have been very kind to an old woman," she said, "very kind." She wrapped the scarf around her neck with the ends hanging down to protect her thin chest. "It is only fitting that I repay your kindness."

He shook his head, bemused. What could *she* possibly give *him*? "That's not necessary, goodfrau," he assured her as her gnarled fingers fumbled under her shawl.

"Oh, but it is," she said. "In this cruel world kindness should always be repaid. So many people passed by me today and yesterday, without a gentle word or a morsel of food. And you have a look about you that I like."

She tugged at something behind her back, and his mouth gaped open. He had taken her for a hunchback, but now she pulled a bundle of cloth out of the back of her dress and held it up.

It was a short cloak, not unlike something an Analousian officer might wear. But instead of the green of the Analousian uniform, this was a dull purple color. It had a high, stiff collar and a gold chain to fasten it. The crone shook it, and Galen saw that it was lined with a pale gray silk.

"You should wear this yourself to keep warm," he said.

The crone cackled. "What, and be run over by a farm wagon? It's madness to travel in such a thing!"

Galen pursed his lips. The poor old woman really was quite out of her head. He wondered if he should help her to the next village. Surely someone would recognize her; she couldn't have wandered far, at her age.

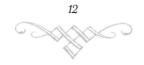

She leaned forward and said in a loud whisper, "It's an invisibility cloak, boy. Try it."

He looked around helplessly, but there was neither cottage nor barn to be seen in any direction. "I really shouldn't—Perhaps we should find your family."

"Try it!" She shrieked like an angry crow and flapped the cloak at him. "Try it!"

He held up his hands in surrender. "All right." He took the cloak from her gingerly and threw it about his shoulders. It caught on his pack and he pulled it free impatiently. "There! How do I look?" He held out his arms. As nearly as he could tell, he was not invisible.

Rolling her eyes, the crone shook her head. "You must *fasten* it."

Not wanting to upset her again, Galen took the dangling end of the chain and fastened it to the gold clasp on the collar. He made to flourish the edges of the cape for dramatic effect but gave a yell instead. He couldn't see his arms. Looking down, he couldn't see any part of himself at all: only two footprints in the dust.

The old woman clapped her hands in delight. "Wonderful! It fits like a dream!"

"I'm invisible," Galen said wonderingly. He walked in a circle, watching his footprints in the dust.

"So you are, but listen to me, boy. It's dangerous being invisible." For the first time she sounded truly lucid, following his footprints with her eyes. "You can be trampled by horses

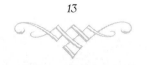

or countless other things. This cloak is not to be used lightly, but only in times of real need."

Galen unfastened the cloak and watched his body ripple into view. With great reluctance he tried to hand the cloak back to the old woman. "I couldn't take something like this from you, goodfrau," he said respectfully. "This is a magical treasure of some kind. You should guard it carefully, or find a magician or some such to sell it to. You could buy yourself a new dress, a cottage even, with the money from something like that."

The crone slapped him before he could duck. "The cloak is not for sale, no matter if I starve to death. It's to be given to the one who needs it most. And that's you, soldier."

He shook his head to clear away the sting from her slap. "But I have no need for it," he said, trying again to give it back. "I'm just a soldier, as you say, or at least I was. I don't have a home or a sweetheart or even work."

Pushing his hands away, the old woman cocked her head to one side. "You'll need this, and more." Again she rummaged among her rags, and this time pulled forth a large ball of white wool and a smaller one of black. "The black is coarse, but strong," she said. "The white is soft, but warm and strong in its own way. One can bind, the other protect. Black like an iron chain, white like a swan floating on the water." She pressed them into his hands, and he nearly dropped the wool and the cloak. "Black like iron, white like a swan," she repeated, staring meaningfully into his face.

Without thinking, he repeated her words. "One can bind, the other protect. Black like iron, white like a swan."

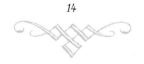

She turned and began walking in the direction Galen had just come from. "You will have need of it, Galen," she said. "When you are in the palace, you will have great need. *He* must not be allowed above."

"Who must not be allowed? And I'm not going to the palace," he said to her retreating back, confused. "I'm going to find work with my aunt and uncle, they—" He broke off. "How did you know my name?"

"Remember, Galen," she called over her shoulder. "When you are in the palace, you will have great need."

Bruch

Galen reached Bruch a week later. The city was much like an army camp: bustling people and mud and the smell of smoke and horses and a thousand other odors, all warring with one another. Unlike the lines of tents, however, the streets of Bruch did not run straight, and Galen soon became confused. Finally he stood in the middle of a street, turning around and around, trying to decide where to go next.

"Lost, soldier?" A stout woman in an apron had come out of a pastry shop nearby. She gave him a warm smile. "Care for a sticky bun?"

His stomach growled loudly, and a girl passing with a basket on her arm giggled. He looked at her, and she looked back boldly and winked.

"I'll take that as a yes," the pastry cook said, drawing his attention back to her. "Come in, come in."

Blushing, Galen went. He didn't want to yell across the street that he had no money to pay for a sticky bun, but the pastry cook stopped him with a hand on his arm before he had taken two steps into her shop.

"I'd not take your money, even if you had any," she said, her kind eyes twinkling at him. "My sons-in-law returned home safe two weeks ago. The day I saw them coming up the road I made a vow that any soldier who came my way would be welcome to eat his fill." Her smile faded a little, and she brushed at some dust on Galen's sleeve. "There's many who have no mother or wife to welcome them open armed, as my daughters' husbands did."

Galen returned her sad smile. "That's a great kindness, goodfrau. My name is Galen Werner."

"I'm Frau Weiss, but you may call me Zelda."

She sat him down at a little table and brought him not only a plate of sticky buns but also a cup of rosehip tea, a large wedge of cheese-and-onion pie, and a glass of cool milk. He thanked her profusely and tucked in, stopping only to rise and be introduced to her two dimpled daughters.

"Our husbands found work right away," the eldest, Jutta, told him in between waiting on customers. "They're repairing the cathedral roof. You'll find something just as quick, I'm sure. It's been hard, with all the able-bodied men gone to war."

The younger sister, Kathe, sniffed. "We made do. I repaired the leak in our roof myself, if you recall."

"And nearly fell to your death on your way back to solid ground, as *I* recall," said Zelda, coming in with a tray of raisin-filled cookies. She slid three onto Galen's plate and then put the rest in the window of the shop.

"Have you any family here in Bruch, Galen?" Zelda stopped by his table again. "Judging by the way you're tucking in, I'd say that you haven't reached home yet."

Feeling guilty about his bad manners, Galen swallowed the rest of his cookie too fast and choked. Jutta pounded him on the back, and her younger sister brought him water.

"Afraid not," he wheezed when he could breathe again. "I don't have a home. I never did: my father was a soldier, and my mother was a laundress with the army. They're both dead. But Mother had a sister in Bruch, and I'm here looking for her."

"Oh, eh?" The widowed baker nodded her head. "What's the name? I've lived in Bruch all my life."

"If Mother hasn't heard of her, she doesn't exist," Kathe said with a snort.

Galen gave her a little bow. "Then I'm very fortunate that I caught your notice, goodfrau," he said. "Mother's sister married an Orm—Reiner Orm. My aunt's name is Liesel."

Kathe's mouth made a little O of surprise. Zelda grunted, looking him over with renewed interest. "I see."

Galen felt a surge of embarrassment. Were his mother's family famously disreputable? She hadn't talked about them all that much. Maybe they were horse thieves or drunkards or some such, and here he had proudly said their name in this respectable shop.

Jutta gave a low whistle. "The *Orms* are your kinfolk? *Reiner Orm?*"

Kathe let out another snort. "Well, at least we can tell you for certain that they'll have work for you. And a place to sleep."

"Hold your tongue, girl," Zelda said, frowning at her younger daughter. She nodded at Galen. "I know the street where Reiner Orm lives," she told him. "Jutta can take you there. The house will be easy enough to find."

"I could take him," Kathe complained.

"You should go in the back and start cooking dinner for your husband," Zelda snapped. "Jutta is less likely to gossip on the way there and dawdle on the way back." The pastry cook went over to Galen and took his hand in hers. "You are welcome anytime, my lad. And should you see any of your companions from the war, tell them to come to the Weisses' shop, and they will be treated to raisin cookies too."

"Thank you, goodfrau . . . Zelda." He stood, still holding her hand, and gave her a bow. "You have been very kind, and I haven't tasted such fine baking . . . well, ever." It was true: his mother had not been known for her cooking.

Zelda blushed and smiled, and told him again to come back. Then she hurried into the kitchen to take care of something in the oven, dragging her sulky younger daughter with her.

Alone, Jutta and Galen exchanged awkward smiles. He lifted his heavy pack to his back without embarrassing himself by groaning, and Jutta led the way out the door and down the street. They walked for quite a distance in silence, until they were within sight of the palace. The palace was tall and angular, with diamond-paned windows like the common houses of Bruch, but it was the size of four houses put together and the walls were of pink stucco, making it look like an ornate confection resting in the center of the city.

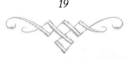

Finally Galen got up the courage to ask about the Orms. "Is there something wrong with them?" he blurted out.

"Wrong with whom?" Jutta looked startled at the outburst.

"With my mother's kin. The Orms. Your mother—your sister—their faces when I said the name..." His voice trailed off.

Jutta laughed aloud, and then, seeing his continued discomfort, she stopped and put a hand on his sleeve. "There is nothing wrong with your family," she said firmly. "It's just that they are well known throughout Bruch. It was quite startling to have one of their relatives wander into our humble shop. I'm sure we all thought that you would say so-and-so, they own a tailor's shop, and we would try to find out where they lived. But to be Reiner Orm's nephew? Goodness!"

"But why are they well known?"

"They weren't before the war," Jutta said. She continued walking, then, so that Galen could not look directly into her face. "Their work was known, of course, known to all of Bruch, but the family itself was not that notable." She softened this statement with a quick smile. "But then ... well, something happened, and there was a great deal of gossip."

Galen stopped in his tracks. He knew it! There was some scandal attached to his mother's cousins. Well, he wasn't sure that he wanted to get tangled up in it.

"It's nothing that will affect you," Jutta said, taking his arm and leading him on. She bit her lip. "I hate to carry tales, and heaven knows that I'm not privy to the whole story, but I can assure you that your family is not defamed."

"Then what happened?"

"It's not for me to say."

And that is all she *would* say as they walked along in awkward silence. They passed a storyteller surrounded by a group of children and shared a smile as the man spun the tale of the Four Princesses of Russaka.

"The king and queen of Russaka had four beautiful daughters," the storyteller proclaimed. "Their hair was bright as gold, their eyes like sapphires, and their lips like the ripest cherries. Wanting to protect them from any evil, the king and queen locked their daughters in a high tower, to which their mother alone had the key. No man ever saw them, and they spent their days singing and embroidering cloths for the church altar. Yet one dark, terrible night, wails were heard coming from the tower. The king and queen unlocked the door, ran up the thousand stairs, and entered the princesses' chamber. There they saw their four sweet daughters, each with a black-haired babe in her arms. "What man has done this?" their father demanded. But the princesses would not say. Then a great shadow covered the moon, and when it had slipped away, the babes were gone. Gone to live deep below the earth, with the creature who was their sire, that black magician whose name is never spoken."

The children listening could be heard squealing with gleeful fright as Galen and Jutta turned a corner and came to a row of houses that faced the western wall of the palace grounds. These were tall, grand houses, with white stucco walls painted with flowers and birds. Halfway along the street, one of the houses stood taller than all the rest, with pink stucco the exact color of the palace and bright green shutters. Window boxes full of white and red geraniums sat beneath each window, and there was a large brass knocker in the middle of the green door. Above the door was a garland of withered ivy twined with a black ribbon: there had been a death in the house. Although, judging by the state of the ivy, it had been some time ago. It was not an unusual sight on this or any other house, however, thanks to the war.

"This is the Orm house," Jutta said, stopping in front of it.

Galen gaped at the imposing house, his stomach dropping into his boots. "Are you certain?" He was convinced that Jutta had made a mistake: his mother's family couldn't possibly live in a house that grand.

"The Orm family has special permission to use the same stucco that is used on the palace," Jutta replied. She patted his arm. "I'll leave you here, Galen. But you're always welcome at the shop."

Galen swallowed. "Thank you. And, er, my best to your husband." Galen bowed.

Jutta gave him a dimpled smile in return and walked away. Galen stood on the pavement in front of the pink house, feeling more lost than he had been before Zelda had called him off the street.

He was about to turn away, to find a kind innkeeper somewhere who would take in a lonely soldier while he screwed up his courage to face his kin, when the green door opened. A woman in a brown dress and fresh white apron stepped out, a basket over her arm. When she saw him, in his blue army tunic and with his pack on his back, she froze and her face went white.

Thinking that she might faint, Galen rushed forward. He took the basket and set it down, not sure what else to do.

"Oh, goodness! Oh, my heart!" She clutched at her ample bosom. "Oh, goodness gracious!" She gasped and then looked at his face again, searchingly. A flicker of disappointment, and of sorrow, played across her face. "I'm so sorry! I thought you were . . . you were . . . someone else." Her eyes flew to the mourning garland over the door, and she swayed on her feet. Galen hastened to ease her down to sit on the top step.

"Take a deep breath, goodfrau," he said, alarmed. "And another deep breath. I'm so sorry to have startled you like that."

"It was not your fault," she assured him. "It was only my own foolishness." She let out a deep sigh. "Oh, dear." Another sigh. Galen patted her hand weakly and she gave him a ghost of a smile. "If you could just help me up?"

Galen helped the woman to her feet and handed her the discarded basket. She seemed to be recovering: her face was no longer as pale, and her breath came easier.

"Please let me apologize again." Galen wanted to crawl into a hole and die. This was probably his aunt's housekeeper, and he'd nearly caused her to have an attack of apoplexy on the doorstep. He couldn't possibly impose on the Orms' hospitality now.

But now that she was on her feet, the woman wasn't going to let him get away. She looked him up and down with frank

eyes, much the same way that Zelda had. "Just getting back from the war, are you?"

"Yes, goodfrau."

"Where's home, then?" She squinted at his face. "You look familiar," she said slowly. "Are you the Bergens' boy?"

"Ah, no."

"The Engels'?"

"No." Galen shifted his feet awkwardly.

"Who are your parents, then?"

Galen drew a deep breath. "My name is Galen Werner. My father was Karl Werner. My mother was Renata Haupt Werner." He rushed onward. "They're both dead. I came here because . . . because this is the only family I have left. I think." He pointed to the pink house.

"Oh!" The woman threw down her basket and wrapped her arms around Galen. "I knew you had a familiar look! Renata's boy! Renata's only boy!"

Awkwardly Galen tried to pat her back. His upper arms were pinned to his sides and she was dragging his pack down with her fierce embrace.

"I'm your mother's sister," the woman said, pulling away at last. She wiped her eyes with a large handkerchief. "Oh, what a pleasure this is! What a surprise! I'm your Tante Liesel."

Waves of relief passed over Galen. This was an even warmer welcome than he had hoped for. She hugged him again, and this time he returned it heartily.

The door opened, and a tall, broad-shouldered man stood there. He frowned at the scene before him. He had gray hair

24

and an impressive mustache that made him look like an angry walrus.

"Liesel, have you taken leave of your senses?"

"Oh, Reiner! Only see: it's dear Renata's boy! He's come home from the war!" She gave Galen a little shove in the back, pushing him toward Reiner Orm.

"How do you do, *meinherr*," Galen said, bowing. "I'm Galen Werner; Karl and Renata Werner were my parents."

"Dead, are they?" Reiner grunted. "Dead in the war?"

"Er, yes, sir." Galen blinked a little at the bluntness of his uncle's words. "My mother died of the lung sickness. Father was shot. My sister, Ilsa, was killed in an accident. Years ago, I'm afraid."

"Oh, the poor darlings! Renata, dead? I never knew!" Liesel clucked and fussed around him, but Galen never took his eyes off Reiner.

Reiner, in return, never took his eyes off Galen. "So, you claim to be Galen Werner, do you?"

"I *am* Galen Werner, sir," Galen replied, not all that surprised to be thus challenged.

"Prove it." Reiner crossed his arms over his chest.

"Reiner, not here," Liesel said, her voice suddenly sharp. She stopped fluttering around Galen and gave her husband a cold look. "The neighbors have talked about us quite enough." She took Galen's arm. "Come inside and have some tea, Galen, while Reiner argues with you."

"Thank you," Galen said doubtfully.

Reiner stepped aside so that Galen and Liesel could enter

the house. Liesel led the way into a well-furnished sitting room and showed Galen to a chair by the hearth. A small fire burned in the grate, and the room was lit with oil lamps. Altogether it was a bright, pleasant room.

Galen set his pack on the floor and took the seat he had been offered. Reiner sat across from him, in a chair that was almost a throne, still raking Galen from head to toe with cold blue eyes. Liesel hurried out and came back a few minutes later with tea, seating herself on a plump little pink chair that had a sewing basket beside it.

Balancing the fine china cup and saucer he had been given on one callused hand, Galen grimly faced his uncle. This was more the welcome he had been expecting, but now that it had happened he was at a loss. How to prove who he was? He had never met these people and his mother had spoken only rarely of her family, who had not approved of her marriage.

Inspiration struck. "I have my father's rifle," he said. He put his tea on a small table and went to his pack. He had wrapped the weapon carefully in canvas against the weather, as was customary on long marches. The bayonet was sheathed and stowed away with the powder and shot. He did not intend to fire it ever again.

The weapon was old and worn, but carefully polished. The burled oak stock had been smoothed by his father's hands, and then his own, until it had a mirror sheen. And carved into the butt was his father's name.

He showed the rifle, and the name, to Reiner. Reiner handled the weapon expertly, but with a disdainful expression. He

grunted and handed it back to Galen when he was done looking it over. "You might have simply stolen Karl's rifle."

"Reiner!" Liesel looked shocked.

"I also have this." Galen rummaged around in his pack, putting his arm in up to the shoulder to take out a small pouch. In it were his parents' wedding rings, simple bands of gold that could have belonged to anyone, and his mother's locket and crucifix. He showed the locket to Reiner and Liesel. It had his mother's initials on the back, and two pictures inside. One of his father, and the other of himself at age eight, holding his infant sister. The crucifix was small and silver, and had the date of his mother's confirmation etched on one side.

Judging by the look on Reiner's face, however, he still thought that Galen was nothing more than a very clever thief. Desperate, Galen racked his brain for other proofs of his identity.

"My mother said that I was named after her grandfather, Galen Haupt, who used to frighten you both by taking out his wooden teeth and hiding them under your pillow, Tante Liesel." Galen thought of another story and blushed but decided to use it anyway. "And, sir, when you were first courting Tante Liesel, you used to slip into the kitchens and eat sweets, and you . . . were very . . . fat." He finished in a rush. "Mother said she used to call you Roly-poly Reiner." Galen put down his parents' things and took a sip of tea, carefully not looking at stern, mustached Reiner Orm.

"So, you're Karl and Renata's son," Reiner said, as if Galen had only just now showed up on his doorstep. He set his own

tea aside. "Get some wine, why don't you, Liesel? We should celebrate the arrival of our nephew." He didn't sound as if he took much pleasure in the idea.

"Indeed we should," Liesel said with exasperation. She gave Galen a peck on the cheek as she passed him.

Reiner grunted. "I suppose you should meet your cousin. We have a daughter, Ulrike. Our son is dead." He went to the door of the sitting room and roared, "Ulrike, come down here!"

Ulrike arrived at the same time as her mother, blinking dreamily. She was a pretty girl, about sixteen years of age, with a good figure and long blond hair. She smiled at Galen. "I'm sorry. I was reading a book." She took a glass of wine from her mother without asking about the occasion.

"You're always reading a book," her father muttered.

"This is your cousin Galen," Tante Liesel explained to Ulrike. "He's coming to stay with us. His parents, my sister and her husband, died in the war."

Ulrike's fair brow clouded. "I'm sorry." She noticed his blue tunic for the first time. "Did you fight in the war, too?"

"Yes. Yes, I did."

"You're very lucky that you weren't killed."

"Yes, I am." Galen looked awkwardly at his wine.

"Did you ever meet—"

Reiner interrupted her with his toast. "To family! And to the family business!" He raised his glass high and they all joined him.

After they had drunk their wine, Ulrike persisted. "Did you know anyone by the name of—"

"Ulrike," Uncle Reiner said, interrupting her again. "Don't pester the boy. You know that I want no talk of the war in this house."

"If my presence bothers you, I can go," Galen said between gritted teeth. It rankled deeply that people who had never seen a battle should have such a strong aversion to the war. He'd actually seen people cross to the other side of the street to avoid passing him, and a man had spit at the sight of a crippled soldier begging outside the city gates.

"Of course your presence doesn't bother us." Reiner seemed genuinely surprised at the idea. "But in this house, we do not speak of the war. My son, Heinrich, is dead because of it." Reiner pointed to the mantel with his wineglass.

There was a small oval picture there, with a wisp of black silk draped across it. Galen lifted the silk and looked at the picture. It was a portrait of a young man near his own age. He was standing beside a chair in the usual stiff posture of such portraits. He wore a dark suit and had his hair neatly combed, yet the artist had managed to capture what seemed to be a glint of mischief in his eyes.

"You can have Heinrich's old room," Tante Liesel said, her voice a bit muffled. When Galen turned around, he saw that she was dabbing her eyes, and Ulrike was looking into the distance and turning her wineglass around and around in her hands.

"Thank you." Galen cleared his throat. "I don't want to be a burden, though. I'd like to find work right away." He had never been idle in his life, and the thought of it filled him with

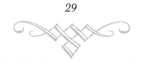

a sense of panic. Even if he had not felt beholden to his uncle, he would have wanted to start work soon. "I don't know if you have need of an extra pair of hands, Uncle Reiner . . . ?"

He felt just as anxious about this as he had about anything so far. He could turn his hand to anything, as long as he was given a chance to learn, but with so many men returning home, there would be a glut of unskilled laborers clamoring for work. He could read and write and do sums, but that was the extent of his education, and he doubted there was much need for a man who could knit a sock in four hours.

But Reiner nodded. "I've needed someone since Heinrich left. You'll do well enough. Just as long as you're careful with your feet, and don't trample His Majesty's pansies."

Galen felt his eyebrows shoot up. What was his uncle talking about? "Sir, I don't quite follow. . . ."

"Don't you know?" Ulrike gave a little laugh. "Papa is the king of the Folly!"

"What?" Galen still didn't understand.

"Ulrike!" Tante Liesel looked shocked. "You shouldn't say such things!"

Reiner shook his finger at his daughter. "It's the king's so-called Folly that keeps clothes on your back and food on the table, not to mention buys those books you spend all your time with." He turned away from his daughter to look at Galen. "Our family has the very great honor of being King Gregor's own gardeners," Reiner said with obvious pride.

Princess

Rose bit her lip as she stood before her father. King Gregor was not happy. He was so very much not happy that a vein on his left temple throbbed and his face was nearly purple.

"This, this, this!" He waved the worn dancing slipper under her nose, unable to say anything else. "This!"

She heard one of her sisters snicker, and nudged the next in line, Lily, with her elbow. Lily passed the nudge on until it reached the snickerer. Poppy, probably. The thirteen-year-old thought everything hilarious of late. Rose wished that Poppy would follow her twin's example more often. Daisy was a model child.

"Do you think this is funny?" King Gregor whirled away from Rose and turned his attention to Poppy, who apparently was the snickerer, as Rose had suspected. "Do you find this amusing?"

"N-n-no, Papa," Poppy stammered.

Rose closed her eyes and prayed for strength. Poppy wasn't

stammering from fright, but from the effort of not laughing aloud. Curse the girl! There really was nothing funny about their situation, and yet Poppy found every opportunity to make light of it.

"Kingdom in a shambles! No money! Wounded soldiers everywhere I look!" King Gregor threw the slipper at the wall in frustration. "And night after night you girls sneak off and do who-knows-what, and expect me to pay for more *fripperies!*"

"No, Father," Rose said.

"What?" The king turned back to his eldest daughter. "Are you saying that you aren't sneaking off? I have the evidence right here!" Now the slipper's mate was waved under her nose. It was one of Orchid's, pink satin with silver ribbons. There was a hole in the toe and one of the ribbons dangled by a thread.

"No, Father," Rose said, remaining as calm as she could. "I'm not denying the evidence. I only meant that you shouldn't have to pay for our 'fripperies.' We will pay for new slippers ourselves, out of our pin money."

The other girls all groaned, but Rose's offer deflated the king somewhat. "Well!" He huffed. "Well! It's not as if you could expect much pin money anyway. Not with the state of affairs this country is in."

"You must not worry, Father," Hyacinth said gravely. She stepped out of line—King Gregor insisted that his daughters line up like soldiers to take their punishments—and held out her hands to their father. Hyacinth was only fifteen, but already she had the pale, serious face and painfully thin body of an ascetic. She spent her days in the chapel, praying for all their

sins, and for their deliverance. She was, surprisingly, an exquisite dancer.

King Gregor did not take Hyacinth's outstretched hands. Instead he glared at her. "You! You have the most sense of all of them, or so I thought! How did they convince you to do this?" He waved the slipper in her face now. "And how is it that you get out of your rooms to begin with? I lock you in every night my own self! Hey? Hey? Answer me! Put you in different rooms, and I wake to find all the doors open and you all lying about the rug in Rose's sitting room like a litter of puppies! What was that about, hey?"

But Hyacinth just bowed her head and backed into line again. Rose heard Hyacinth sigh. She couldn't tell the truth, and Hyacinth would never lie.

"You may well sigh, my girl," Gregor said. Then he softened, most of his ire having been worked out by the shouting. "Now, be off with you all. I will have Herr Schmidt come and make you a new set of dancing slippers. You'll need them: Breton's new ambassador will be arriving this afternoon. But the cost *will* come out of your pin money," he warned. "It will have to," he muttered under his breath as he walked away.

"Poor Father," Lily said when he was out of earshot. "Things are so very bad these days and to have *this* to contend with makes it even worse."

"I don't want new slippers," Petunia said. She was the youngest, at six. "I want to buy sweets, and then I shall dance barefoot!" And she began to twirl around the room. "La, la-la, la!"

Pansy, who was seven, sat down on the floor with a flump.

33

"I don't want new slippers either. I don't want to dance anymore!" And she began to cry.

"There, there!" Lily rushed to her side and picked up the little girl. Their hair was the same shade of glossy brown and both wore blue dresses today. Pansy liked to match clothes with her favorite sister.

"I'm sorry, sweeting," Rose said, rubbing Pansy's back. "But you know that we have to dance."

"Now I can't have the new music I wanted to buy," Violet grumped. At fourteen, she was a prodigy on the pianoforte and sang like an angel. "I have to pay for dancing slippers instead!"

"I'm sorry," Rose said automatically.

She felt like she was always apologizing these days: for wearing out her slippers, for her sisters' exhaustion, for the poverty of the country. And none of it was her fault. "I'm sorry." And then, rather than have to see eleven pairs of sad eyes looking at her any longer, she walked away. She was the oldest, and their mother had charged her with caring for her sisters, but sometimes the burden was too great.

Rose went out of the long gallery where she and her sisters had been assembled, down a flight of steps, and through the tall doors that led to her mother's garden. Once in the garden, she paused to breathe deeply. The palace smelled of stone and paint, of people and food and beeswax floor polish.

The garden smelled only of flowers and earth.

Her mother, Queen Maude, had been from Breton and had not liked the cold, harsh winters of Westfalin. She hadn't

liked the dark evergreen trees or the scruffy little edelweiss flowers and holly bushes that had comprised the palace garden before she came, either.

To make his new bride happy, King Gregor had ordered the old garden redone. Flowers from Breton had been imported, along with ornamental trees, climbing vines, and even Bretoner-made iron benches and marble statuary, all to make Maude feel at home.

Unfortunately, Westfalin and Breton did not share the same climate. The gentle misting rains of Breton, the soft winter snows and warm, humid summers transformed in Westfalin into freezing sleet, blizzards, and summers so hot and dry that many less hardy plants perished. In order to keep the Queen's Garden flourishing, a team of gardeners had to work daily, watering, weeding, fertilizing, and coaxing the tea roses, lilacs, and ivy.

It seemed only natural when the queen named her daughters after the flowers in her garden, calling them her own garden of lovelies. But then, when little Petunia was only two years old, Queen Maude died. In memory of his beloved wife, King Gregor kept her garden exactly as it had been.

This caused no little resentment among the Westfalian people. The kingdom had been at war for more than six years, and there had already been protests over the extravagance that was the Queen's Garden. It was thought wasteful to spend the manpower and the resources to keep the garden flourishing, and the queen's death was seen by some as a reason to put a stop to what had become known as Gregor's Folly.

But King Gregor did not dig up his wife's roses to plant wheat. There were no potatoes among the daisies, nor carrots in the primroses. It was still a pleasure garden, even when there was little pleasure to be had outside the palace walls.

Rose was grateful for the garden. Not only for the reminder it provided of her gentle mother, but also for the privacy it afforded. Here were endless paths that wound between shielding trees. There were bowers of climbing roses, artfully trained to arch over benches where a girl might sit and think, out of sight of her sisters, her governess, and maids. There were always gardeners at work, but the head gardener, Reiner Orm, was not a talkative man and did not hire gossips to work for him. They respected the privacy of the royal family, and left them alone.

As she rounded a corner, Rose came upon one of the under-gardeners. Walter Vogel was a grizzled man with sparkling blue eyes and a wooden leg. He had showed up at the gates of the palace on the day Rose was born, looking for work, and by now was as much a fixture of palace life as the king. Walter was seated on a boulder, his wooden leg propped on his good knee, and his chin propped on a fist.

"Good morning, Walter," Rose said.

"Good morning, Princess Rose," he said gravely. "I was just sitting for a moment and pondering the state of the world."

"I see." She smiled a little. It was very like Walter to say such obscure things, but she really wanted to be alone. She began edging past.

He climbed down off the boulder. "But if I don't get to work pruning the weeping cherry tree, I'll need to worry about the state of my hide." He winked at her and picked up his pruning shears.

Rose held a finger to her lips. "I won't breathe a word, should I see Master Orm," she promised.

"Thank you kindly, Princess Rose," Walter said. "O' course, the master gardener's caught up with training a newcomer. Seems his nephew returned from the war yesterday. A fine young man, but he can't tell a lilac from a peony."

Rose nodded in sympathy.

"They're down that-a-way," Walter said, jerking his thumb to the left. "You might want to take your ease by the swan fountain, Princess, instead of the yellow-rose bower." He was well acquainted with Rose's favorite haunts.

"Thank you, Walter," she said, and turned toward the fountain.

He saluted her with the shears as she passed.

Rose went along the westward path until she came to the swan fountain. It was one of the smaller ones, though the bowl below the statue of the larger-than-life swan was still large enough to bathe in. The bird's bronze neck curved over the floating lilies, its beak just touching the clear water. There were benches all around the fountain, and it was on one of these Rose liked to sit and think. The palace peacocks, with their strange creaking cries, could be heard only faintly from here, making it a place of quiet reflection.

Literally. Rose could look through the clear water and see her image in the burnished bottom of the fountain. She wished that Master Orm and his gardeners weren't quite so conscientious about keeping it clean. There was something disturbing about looking into the water and seeing a vision of your drowned self looking back.

Rose tucked a loose strand of hair behind her ear. She hadn't realized that she looked so tired. She was barely seventeen years old but thought she looked much older. She stirred the water with a finger, breaking up the image, and turned her back on the fountain to gaze out over the garden.

Why shouldn't she appear tired? She had eleven younger sisters all looking to her for guidance. She had taken her mother's place as the designated hostess for all social functions at the palace, and there had been a great many lately in the wake of the victory against Analousia. Just now there were three different foreign ambassadors at the palace, being wined and dined and hopefully signing lucrative trade agreements.

And almost every night there was the dancing.

There was always dancing after state dinners, and as the crown princess she was never "humiliated" by having to sit out a dance without a partner. King Gregor believed that an excess of revelry was unwholesome, however, so the dancing always ended promptly at eleven o'clock.

Which gave the twelve sisters just enough time to freshen up before they attended the Midnight Ball.

Rose turned back to the water and leaned over to look at her

reflection again. Did it show on her face that she was cursed? Tired, yes, she certainly appeared tired. But would a curse—her curse, her sisters' curse, her mother's curse—leave its mark too?

A sudden scuffling of the gravel on the path startled her, and she lost her balance, slipping headfirst into the water. But before she could crack her skull on the bottom of the fountain, a strong arm was around her waist, pulling her back.

"Easy, there! Easy!"

Sputtering, Rose found herself back on her favorite bench, only now she was sopping wet and embarrassed besides. A tall, rather handsome young man was standing over her, looking concerned. His brown gardening smock was open at the collar, despite the chill in the air, and she could see a thin white scar slashing the tanned skin it revealed. Curious, she couldn't stop staring at this.

"Um, *fraulein?*"

His voice drew her gaze upward. His voice was young, but his face was tanned from long hours in the sun, and there were even a few lines at the corners of his eyes and mouth. His hair was very short, but looked like it might curl if given the chance.

"*Fraulein?* Are you all right? Did I frighten you?"

Rose stopped staring and mustered her dignity. Of course he had startled her—she hadn't suddenly decided to dive into an icy fountain for her health!—but she felt it would be rude to mention that. Instead she nodded graciously.

"Thank you for your help," she said, trying to ignore the cold water that was dripping off her hair and soaking her

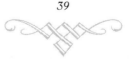

dress, or the fact that most of her shawl was still in the fountain, with only a corner of it hooked over her elbow.

"I'm Galen," the young man said, picking up the rake he had dropped to help her. He held out his free hand.

Rose looked at him in shock. Did he not know who she was? True, the Westfalian court was rather informal, but princesses did not shake hands with gardeners in any country she had heard of. Then it occurred to her that he must be the new gardener, Master Orm's nephew.

"Oh!" She stood but didn't take his hand. "I'm Princess Rose," she explained, smiling stiffly. She knew what would happen next: he would turn red, and then start stammering, and then back away. And whenever she passed him in the future, the awkward dance would be repeated.

He did turn red, but just a little, and his tan hid most of it. But instead of stammering and backing away, he gave her a bow and simply said, "A pleasure to meet you, Your Highness. Please forgive me for not recognizing you."

Now Rose was the one stammering. "Quite—quite all right. No harm done . . . Galen."

"Do you need help getting back to the palace, Your Highness? The weather is quite chill, and you took a good dunking there."

"Um, no, thank you." She dragged her shawl out of the fountain and gathered the heavy, dripping mass together as best she could. "I'll be fine, thank you."

He nodded courteously. "I'd better finish raking, then," he said.

"Yes."

He was still looking at her.

"Yes?" Now she was even more flustered and confused.

"If I have your leave to go, Your Highness . . . ?"

"What? Oh! Of course." She nodded her head and then, feeling foolish, made her escape. "Good-bye!" She walked quickly down the path that led to the palace.

After he was out of sight, she slowed down a little. The princesses did not require people to ask permission to leave; it was more the king's prerogative.

"But where did he learn such nice manners?" she wondered aloud.

"What did you say, Rose?" Lily came around a hedge and stared at her. "Why are you all wet?"

"I'm not *all* wet," Rose said irritably. "I'm *partly* wet. I fell in the fountain. The swan fountain. A gardener had to fish me out and . . . what are you doing?"

Lily was holding a basket full of handkerchiefs. Rose looked around and realized that they were at the entrance to the hedge maze. A chill breeze came rushing around them, rattling the autumn-dry hedge and making her shiver.

"Oh, it's the younger set." That was how the three youngest sisters—Orchid, Pansy, and Petunia—were referred to by the others. Rose, Lily, and Jonquil were the "older set," and the six in the middle were "in-betweeners." "They wanted to play Hansel and Gretel, so I'm leaving a trail of handkerchiefs for them. Except the handkerchiefs keep blowing away."

"We wanted to use white rocks," Orchid chimed in, popping

around the corner and startling Rose. "But Lily said that Master Orm would be angry if we rearranged his rocks. Do you think that he would? And aren't they Papa's rocks anyhow?"

"They wanted to use the pebbles from the main path," Lily explained. "I was mostly worried that the rocks would chip the blades of the grass clippers, when they trim the lawn next."

"A good idea," Rose said, and then sneezed. "Oh dear, I'd best get inside."

"Why are you all wet?" Orchid blinked up at her owlishly.

"I'm not all wet," Rose said again. "I put my arm in a fountain."

"And your head and your other arm and your shawl," Orchid pointed out. "Which fountain was it? Was the water very cold?"

"The swan fountain, and yes it was," Rose answered her. "Now why don't we all go inside? It's too chilly to play out here."

"Yes, *Mother*." Orchid rolled her eyes.

Rose didn't bother to reply. Being called "Mother" on top of being cold, and wet, and upset about well, everything, had set her temper on the boil. She stamped off to the palace with her dripping shawl hanging from her arms. She passed Lilac and the twins, Poppy and Daisy, on her way to the room she shared with Lily and Jonquil. All three opened their mouths to say something but closed them again when they got a good look at Rose's face.

Rose stalked into her room and slammed the door.

Jonquil was brushing her hair in front of the big looking glass above their dressing table. "Can I borrow your blue shawl? Violet and Iris say that the new under-gardener is handsome and I want to go see for myself."

Rose threw her sopping shawl at Jonquil and climbed into bed, wet clothes and all.

Ill

By the time the dinner gong struck, Rose was running a temperature. She lay in her bed, miserable, and coughed into a handkerchief. Lily had seen Rose's wet hair and gown sticking out of the covers, summoned a maid, and forcibly gotten her older sister dried off and into a nightgown. Rose barely noticed.

The shoemaker had brought new dancing slippers, since he knew all their sizes by heart, but she hadn't tried hers on or even looked at them. The poor man was anxious to please—the princesses were his best customers, after all—so Lily assured him on Rose's behalf that the workmanship was once more unsurpassed.

Jonquil, having readily forgiven her older sister for the wet shawl incident, described the slippers to Rose in detail and then picked out a yellow gown for her to wear to supper. "This will match perfectly," she said, holding up the gown where Rose could see it.

Rose hardly bothered to glance at it. Then she sneezed

three times in quick succession and pulled the covers over her head.

"I wish I were dead," she moaned.

Petunia came twirling into the room. "Are you sick?" She danced up to Rose's bedside and peered at her. "You look sick. *I'm* not sick. I'm never sick." She twirled away.

Lily came over and felt Rose's forehead. "I'll send for Dr. Kelling," she said in a worried voice. "You're burning up."

"I can't be sick," Rose said, struggling to get free of the covers. "I can't." But she couldn't even move the heavy comforter off her legs, and fell back against the pillows with a groan. "I wish I were dead," she said again.

Lily sent a message for the royal physician, and Jonquil put Rose's new dancing slippers and the yellow gown away. Her brow was furrowed with anxiety, as was Lily's. They stood on either side of their eldest sister's bed, exchanging looks and restlessly adjusting the covers.

The other girls were gathered in the doorway that connected Rose, Jonquil, and Lily's room to the room shared by Hyacinth, Violet, and the twins. Petunia kept breaking free of Daisy's restraining hands to dance around Rose's bed and sing for her. Hyacinth was praying, and Poppy said something under her breath that made Iris gasp.

"What's all this?" Dr. Kelling arrived and looked around at the gathered sisters in bemusement. "Is this supposed to help?" A wave of his hand took in the dancing Petunia, the hovering older set, and the noise coming from Hyacinth and Poppy. "Is this a sickroom or a zoo? All of you, out!" He

made a shooing gesture at the sisters. "Oh, and Poppy? Mind your language!"

Daisy gathered up the younger set, while Poppy took Hyacinth by the arm with surprising gentleness and led her away. Jonquil and Lily refused to go, however, standing adamantly by Rose's bed.

"Very well," Dr. Kelling grunted. He had been the royal physician for over twenty years and had delivered all twelve of the princesses. "What happened?" As he said this, he took Rose's pulse, then felt her forehead and looked in her mouth.

"She fell into a fountain in the garden," Lily answered, since Rose was busy saying "ah" for the doctor.

"It's much too cold to go swimming, don't you know that?" Dr. Kelling joked. "Looks like you've caught a nasty chill, *liebchen*. Ague, to be certain. We can only pray that it does not turn to pneumonia."

"I believe that Hyacinth is already doing that," Jonquil said, smiling weakly. Through the closed door, they could still hear their sister's murmured prayers, occasionally punctuated by Poppy's shouts for quiet.

"You are not to leave this bed without my permission," Dr. Kelling said with a wry smile for Jonquil's jest. "I shall have a bowl of fresh oranges brought to you from the hothouse. You will eat three a day for the next week at least. Also, I'll give the kitchen orders for some warming broths, and a soothing tea for the cough."

"But the dancing," Rose said, and was racked with a coughing fit that lasted several minutes. When it was over, she didn't even

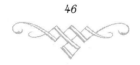

have the strength to keep her eyes open, but lay on the pillow and merely listened as Dr. Kelling told her that under no circumstances was she to leave her bed, let alone dance.

"Lily can sit beside your father and play hostess this evening," Dr. Kelling said kindly, patting Rose's white hand where it lay on the coverlet. "And for the next several nights. But don't worry, I'm sure that she will give you back your place as soon as you are well."

"Of course I will," Lily said. But she didn't even pretend to be cheerful.

"I'm sure that, in light of your illness, your father will cancel the dancing this evening," Dr. Kelling said, "if it will distress you to know that your sisters are making merry while you lie ill in bed."

"Thank you, Dr. Kelling," Rose murmured. "I'll sleep now."

"Good girl." He stroked her damp hair. "I'll tell your father the news and send the orders to the kitchens." Then he leveled his gaze at Jonquil and Lily. "You may want to sleep elsewhere, to prevent yourselves from catching Rose's chill. And try to bar the little ones from the sickroom as well. If all twelve of you fall ill, it will qualify as an epidemic."

Lily and Jonquil smiled dutifully at the joke, and Lily saw him to the door of the room. "Thank you, Dr. Kelling," she said. As soon as she had closed the door behind him, she ran back to Rose's bed and looked down at her sister with anxiety written large on her face. "Rose? Are you still awake?"

"Yes," Rose said, and coughed some more. "Fool gardener, leaping out of the shrubbery and frightening people."

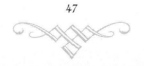

"Rose," Lily said urgently. "What are we to do? About the ball?"

Dr. Kelling had misunderstood Rose when she asked about the dancing. She was not worried about the state dinner, or the dancing that usually followed. She was worried about what came after: the Midnight Ball. King Gregor had no control over that. It would not be canceled due to illness. Death alone could free a soul from the Midnight Ball, as the girls knew all too well.

"There's nothing we can do," Rose said, and a tear slipped out of the corner of her eye and ran down to wet her pillow. "If I don't go, he'll be so angry." She rolled onto her side and pulled the blankets over her head again.

The other eleven princesses dressed for dinner and sat at the long table with their father and the three visiting ambassadors. The girls were nervous and gloomy all night, and King Gregor did indeed cancel the dancing that evening. The sisters kissed their father good night at nine and went upstairs to Rose. Lily helped her sit up and drink a cup of chamomile tea, made with herbs that grew in their own garden. Jonquil peeled two oranges and fed them to Rose one segment at a time.

And then, at eleven o'clock, Lily and Jonquil helped Rose out of bed. They washed her face and applied rouge to her pale cheeks and lips. They combed her long golden-brown hair and put it up in an elegant knot atop her head, adorning it with a tiara of pearls and garnets. Then they helped her into the yellow dress and the new dancing slippers.

The eldest princess could barely walk. She was near delirious

with fever and racked by coughing spells that left her breathless and teary-eyed. Lily and Jonquil had to support her all the way to the Midnight Ball.

⌘

When Maria, their chief maid, came to wake the three eldest princesses the next morning, she found Rose's yellow ball gown on the floor beside her bed, and Queen Maude's pearl-and-garnet jewelry set lying on the bedside table. Rose was insensible with fever, raving about trees of silver and boats of gold crossing a lake of shadows. The maid thought that Rose had, in her delirium, attempted to dress for dinner. Maria woke the other girls and got Rose to drink some cool water while they waited for Dr. Kelling to arrive.

"I don't understand it," Maria clucked, tenderly washing Rose's face with cool water. "It's astounding enough that she managed to get that gown out of the wardrobe, sick as she is. But how did she wear out a new pair of slippers?"

"I don't know," Lily said innocently, kicking her own worn-out slippers under the bed.

Then Jonquil coughed.

Plan

As the princesses succumbed to Rose's illness one by one, King Gregor became desperate. He was a good-hearted man, for all his blustering and arm waving, and it pained him deeply to see his girls suffer. Worse still, Dr. Kelling feared that Rose's illness was turning to pneumonia, and that brought back grief-ripe memories of Queen Maude's last illness.

To add insult to injury, the mystery of the worn-out dancing slippers continued. Every third morning when the king visited his daughters' rooms, it was to find them sicker than ever and with their dancing slippers lying at their bedside, worn to pieces. Gregor accused their maids of stealing his daughters' shoes at night to meet their gentlemen friends, and even fired two of them before the housekeeper could point out that none of the servants could wear the younger girls' shoes.

King Gregor begged and pleaded with his daughters to tell him what was going on, but they refused to answer, standing there coughing piteously and looking hollow eyed. He had hoped to marry one or two of them off to their new allies in Spania and La Belge, perhaps even to smooth things over with Analousia through marriage. But now all the girls were sick (and unattractively so, with red noses and hacking coughs), and the rumors of the constantly worn-out slippers had caught the attention of the city's gossips.

It was Kelling who brought him that unwelcome piece of news. The shoemaker or one of the servants must have talked, because the town was awash with stories about the princesses' nighttime activities. It was being said that they were ill from dancing with the fairy folk. Some even said the girls had caught some strange fairy ailment that could be cured only by dancing even harder than before, or by drinking goat's milk under a blue moon, or other foolishness. Others spitefully whispered that it was God's punishment on King Gregor for the war or for wasting so much money and labor on that fool garden.

The king put his head in his hands. "What am I to do, Wilhelm?" he moaned.

Dr. Kelling put his physician's bag on the king's desk and sat in one of the large leather chairs opposite. His father had been the prime minister during the reign of Gregor's father, and the two had been boys together. They had served in the army side by side, been married the same year, and been widowed within a month of each other.

Feeling nearly as exhausted as his daughters, Gregor leaned back in his tall leather chair. It was like watching his Maude fade away all over again. He promised her he'd take good care of their girls, but she hadn't seemed to believe him. Her eyes

had been filled with such despair toward the end. And last night, visiting with Rose, he'd seen the same look. And why? If they could only show him the root of the trouble, he would seek it out and destroy it. But there was only silence and tears and hopelessness.

"Wilhelm, I . . ." The king's voice trailed away. He didn't know what to say, what to do. When war with Analousia had been inevitable, he had made the decision that had seemed best, and they had triumphed in the end. But how to triumph when you didn't know what battle you were fighting?

Dr. Kelling leaned forward. "We've got to get to the bottom of this, Gregor," he said. "It does no good to ask them; they cannot or will not tell. Now, I'm not one to indulge in talk of fairies and the like, you know that. But it seems to me that something is very wrong here. Something beyond youthful high spirits and a love of dancing." He snorted. "Which doesn't seem to be there, by the way. Poor little Pansy, when she was delirious with fever, kept sobbing that she wanted to stop dancing. God alone knows why they keep it up. Now, Maude was a good woman, but you and I both know that she brought some fanciful ideas over from Breton, along with her love of roses."

"What are you saying?" King Gregor shook his head, confused. "You think Maude had something to do with this?"

"No-o, but . . ." Dr. Kelling scrubbed his hands over his face. "I don't know, Gregor. Perhaps I'm just tired." He sighed heavily. "But Rose grows weaker by the day. I know you've tried separating the girls at night, but have you had them guarded, or followed, to see where they go?"

King Gregor's shoulders slumped. "I want to trust my girls. I feel like their jailer as it is, locking them in at night. Has it come to that?"

"It has, if we are to make Rose well again," Dr. Kelling said gently. "Tonight's the third night since their last . . . disappearance or what-have-you. Separate rooms, and windows and doors firmly latched. Guards in the hallway."

In silence they finished off a decanter of brandy and smoked a number of fine cigars. In the end, King Gregor sighed, stubbed out his last cigar, and nodded.

"Very well. The ambassadors have moved to their manors in the town now. That frees up all the bedrooms on the third floor. You'll stay tonight in case the girls need you?" the king asked.

"Of course."

Gardener

Galen sat on a large rock and knitted a pair of socks. Well, just one sock. He had already made the other the evening before, and was hoping to have this one done before the next day. The socks he had brought back from the war were so worn they had disintegrated when his aunt washed them, and he had spent the past few weeks trying to replace them.

Good-hearted Tante Liesel had offered to knit his new socks, but Galen had politely refused. The truth was, knitting was the only skill he had learned during the war that he enjoyed. There was something soothing about watching stitch after stitch pass across the needles, something meditative about the process. It also gave him a sense of pride to create something, as opposed to the destruction of shooting other men.

His cousin, Ulrike, was fascinated to see a man knitting. "Who would think that a man—and a soldier!—would do such a thing?" she marveled.

"Many soldiers do," he told her. "There is no other way,

on a battlefield, to get new socks or a warm scarf when winter sets in."

"But all of my friends and I knitted endless socks and scarves. Hats and mittens, too," Tante Liesel had protested. "We sent boxes of them to the army! Ulrike made nine stocking caps last winter. Didn't you, *liebchen?*"

Galen shook his head. "I'm sorry, Tante. They went astray somewhere, or there were not enough to go around. I've never had a sock that wasn't knit by my mother or myself."

"Well," his aunt had assured him, "Ulrike and I can keep you in socks and caps now."

But Galen couldn't sit idle. He had spent too many years knitting socks, or polishing weapons or building camps. So every day he slipped his needles and yarn into his satchel, along with the hearty lunch his aunt provided.

"What are you doing, boy?" Uncle Reiner came down the path to stand, frowning, before the rock on which Galen sat with his knitting.

The obvious answer was "knitting," but Galen knew that his uncle would not find that answer amusing. "I'm waiting for Walter to bring the mulch for this bed," Galen said, pointing with one sharp needle at the flower bed nearby. "I offered to help but he insisted on doing it himself."

Walter Vogel had taken Galen in hand after his first day, training him in the use of the various garden tools and teaching him the names and natures of the plants that they cared for. There were nearly a dozen other gardeners under Reiner Orm, who variously regarded their work in the King's Folly as an

embarrassment or a privilege. Either way, they were not that friendly toward the newcomer. Many of them had sought work in the gardens to avoid going to war, and seeing someone they considered a mere boy who had fought while they pruned hedges made them uncomfortable. So Walter made Galen his assistant, and Galen ignored the other gardeners as they ignored him.

Galen and Walter had already trimmed the winter-dead flowers down to dirt level and were preparing to cover them with mulch to protect their roots from the cold. In the past Galen had thought that gardening, like farming, was a matter of luck. You planted something, you watered it, you hoped that it grew.

Here, though, was an intriguing new world. A world of thinning, mulching, bandaging, grafting, and pruning—it was like building fortifications against an enemy invader. Trunks of trees and whole shrubs had to be wound with strips of burlap for the winter. The iris roots or "corms," which looked rather like withered parsnips, were dug up, separated, and then replanted.

Gophers, mice, and other rodents were the bane of the Queen's Garden. The gardeners did double duty as exterminators, keeping an eye out for any signs of burrowing or nibbling. Walter had a pair of small dachshunds that roamed the garden, their liquid brown eyes on the lookout for trespassing vermin. Their sharp barks at finding prey carried clearly over the screeching of the peacocks.

Now as Walter came trundling around the corner with a full wheelbarrow, Galen stowed his knitting in a canvas bag

and jumped down to help. Under the watchful eyes of Reiner Orm, they carefully shoveled a layer of rich black mulch over the stumps of the hollyhocks. Galen overloaded his shovel in his zeal, and a clump of mulch fell on the browning grass.

"The garden must be made ready for winter," Reiner said. "But"—he held up an admonishing finger—"it must still be pleasing to the eye."

"Yes, sir," Galen said, raking up the clump with his fingers and scattering it over the bed.

"There will be a great many important guests this winter. *Royal* guests."

Both Galen's and Walter's heads snapped up, but it was Galen who asked the question. "Is there more trouble? With Analousia?"

"No, lad, nothing like that," Reiner was quick to reassure them. No one wanted another war. "The ambassadors will be coming and going, and I was told that the princesses would be receiving more guests."

"The king is thinking of a royal marriage?" Walter rubbed his chin, looking thoughtful. "Rose, most likely; she's the oldest." His expression clouded. "O' course, she's the most ill right now, poor girl. And there are other things—" He saw Galen and Reiner looking at him and stopped abruptly. "Forgive my rambling."

"Princess Rose is ill?" Galen had wondered why he hadn't seen any of the princesses in the garden since the day that Rose had fallen in the fountain. He felt a surge of guilt. She wouldn't have fallen in if he hadn't startled her, but seeing her

there, with her white face turned toward the bronze swan, had made him think of the crone and her strange gifts.

"Very ill, as are the others. It's the talk of Bruch, and they say that—"

"Walter, Galen," Reiner said stiffly. "We do not speak of the royal family in this familiar fashion." But as he stalked away, they could faintly hear him muttering, "Young ladies running wild, dancing about all night in their rooms. . . ."

Galen drew back and exchanged a look with Walter. Once his uncle was out of earshot, Galen traded his shovel for a rake. "Dancing all night in their rooms?"

"You may be the only person in Bruch who hasn't heard the gossip," Walter told him. They raked for a while in silence, and then the older man spoke. "Every third night the girls emerge from their rooms exhausted, with their dancing shoes in tatters. Dr. Kelling, the royal physician, says this is the cause of their continuing illness."

"But I don't understand," Galen said. "If they are ill, why are they dancing all night? Or are they sneaking out to meet suitors? Can't a guard follow them?" It seemed ludicrous to imagine the king's daughters climbing out their window in the night, attired in ballgowns and dancing slippers, but he supposed stranger things had happened.

"Guards outside the rooms, maids within, and no one sees or hears a thing," Walter said. "Though I understand that last night, extra steps were taken." He frowned. "If they do keep the princesses in their beds, it may be a mixed blessing."

"How so?"

But Reiner had sent one of the other under-gardeners to help, and Walter would say no more in front of the man.

All the while they were busy spreading the black mulch, Galen thought of Princess Rose. She was ill, quite possibly because of the dunking she took the day they met, and something was compelling her to dance night after night. How would she ever rest and recover?

His guilt increased when, later that day, he was assigned to clean stray leaves out of the swan fountain and rake the gravel around its base. He set to it with a will, though. Walter had told him that this was one of Princess Rose's favorite spots, and Galen thought that at the least he could keep it nice for her. Of course, with the weather turning cold and night falling ever earlier, it would likely be some time before the invalid princess could visit.

When Galen was done it was nearly full dark, and he had to make his way slowly to the distant toolshed to return his rake. He nodded to the other gardeners and accepted a lantern to light his way home. Uncle Reiner would stop in briefly at the palace. He and King Gregor were breeding new types of roses in a hothouse on the east side of the gardens, and on days when the king didn't have time to check on their progress, the head gardener reported to him in person.

Walter was standing just outside the toolshed, a troubled look on his seamed face. His lantern hung loosely from one hand, and Galen thought the older man looked to be in danger of dropping it.

"Walter? Are you all right?" Galen took the lantern from him.

"Another gate is open," Walter said in a hoarse voice. "I can feel it."

"What gate?" It was a fifteen-minute walk to the palace gates from the shed. "How can you feel it?"

"Get back in the shed," Walter said. Another of the gardeners was just stepping out with his own lantern. "All of you! Get back!" In a sudden frenzy, the peg-legged man began shoving them all back inside. He slammed the door on them and barred it from the outside.

"What the devil?" Jakob, who had helped Galen and Walter earlier, stared at Galen. "He's run mad!"

Galen felt the back of his neck prickle. The wind had picked up, rattling the shed's small window, and Galen heard dogs howling in the distance.

"Something's wrong," Galen said. He put both lanterns on the tool bench and went to the window, swinging it wide. "Walter! What's happening?" The wind came in and nearly stole his breath, causing Galen to stagger back. From their bed in the corner, Walter's normally fearless dachshunds huddled together, whimpering.

The window was barely wider than his shoulders, but Galen grabbed the sill and shoved himself through. His belt buckle caught for a moment on the frame, and he ended up landing on one shoulder in a flower bed. He quickly rolled to his feet and brushed off the dirt.

"Walter?"

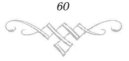

"Galen!" The older man came stumping around the corner. "Stay inside!"

"No, tell me what's happening!"

It was dark, and Galen could barely make out Walter's head shake. "No time, no time! Take this." And he pressed a switch into Galen's hands. "Rowan, best I can do in a pinch."

"For what? The storm?"

The wind was tearing through the gardens, and Galen thought with despair of how many leaves he would have to dredge out of the swan fountain in the morning. Strangely, it didn't smell of rain or snow, both of which were possible at this time of year, but of mold and stone.

"This is no storm," Walter said evenly. "Do you know where the windows of the princesses' sitting room are?"

"The south side? Overlooking the hedge maze?" That he knew this so readily made Galen blush. He hadn't been trying to peep at the princesses, but he'd seen them at those windows more often than at any of the others.

"That's right. Come quickly!"

Walter moved off at greater speed than Galen would have thought a man with a false leg could go. Galen was soon trotting to keep up as the wind buffeted them. They skirted wide around the maze and came upon the smooth lawn on the south side of the palace.

The windows were all ablaze, and Galen could see anxious faces peering out: servants curious about the sudden wind. The princesses' sitting room was on the third floor, and Galen thought he saw movement there.

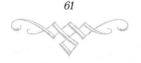

But then his attention was caught by a sound that sliced through the wind. A hollow howling sound that was no dog Galen had ever heard. Strange, creeping shapes were coming out of the hedge maze, from behind a fountain shaped like a mermaid, around the corner of the palace. They were like tall men, stooped over.

"Hey, hallo there," Galen called, his words carried off by the wind. "Hey!"

"Galen!" Walter shouted.

One of the figures lunged at Galen. He brought up his switch just in time and lashed his attacker across the face with it. A surprisingly human cry followed, and the hunched figure fell back. Now more creatures were coming at them, and Galen and Walter whipped at them as best they could.

"Stop there!" With a surge of panic, Galen saw that one of the figures had gone around them and was attempting to climb the ivy on the palace wall. It grew all the way to the princesses' windows, and though it would not hold a grown man's weight, these ... beings ... were slender and seemed almost insubstantial. "I said, *stop!*" Galen rushed after the figure, switching it across the back.

Above them, a window flew open. One of the princesses, her hair streaming in the wind, leaned out.

"I see you, Rionin," she cried, her voice rough. She doubled over, coughing. "I see you!" It was Rose. "Go back, and tell him we're coming." More coughing, and another girl appeared at the window.

Galen heard a familiar click and froze. The second princess

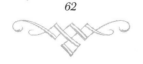

had just cocked a pistol. In the rising moonlight, he could see it in her hand, pointed squarely at the figure Rose called Rionin.

"He's made his point," the second princess said, her voice shaking.

Rionin reached up a hand.

Galen brought his rowan switch down just as the pistol went off. The bullet went over their heads and buried itself in the lawn, but Galen didn't think the princess had meant to hit this Rionin, only warn him.

The figures began to fade back now. Rionin hissed at Galen and then lurched away, hunched in the moonlight and with smoke rising from his back where Galen had struck him.

Walter stumped over and called up to the window, "Your Highnesses, are you all right?"

"Yes, thank you, Walter." The second princess lowered her pistol, rather unsteadily.

"Careful with that," Galen yelped.

"She was taught well," Walter assured him. "Back to bed with you now, young highnesses," Walter called up to the window.

"But only for a few hours," Rose said, drooping against the window frame. "We'll have to go tonight, and it's not even the third night."

"I know," Walter said quietly. The wind had died down, and in the following stillness, the old man's words were clear.

Rose's sister pulled her inside, and they latched the window. Cries could be heard now, and shouts, from inside and outside the palace.

"Walter, what just happened?" Galen's voice shook, but he didn't care. His skin still prickled, and a cold sweat ran down his back.

"The less you know, the better off you are," Walter said. He tossed aside his switch. "Dispose of that properly tomorrow," he grunted. "Moonlight enough to see you home?"

"I—I suppose."

"Good night, Galen." And the old man stumped away, leaving Galen with a sick feeling in his stomach, clutching a rowan switch in the moonlight.

Solution

There were . . . creatures . . . in Maude's garden." With shaking hands, King Gregor reached for the decanter of brandy, but he was too stricken to pour. He drew back and clutched the arms of his leather office chair. "You saw them, Wilhelm."

"I did, indeed," Dr. Kelling agreed gravely.

"Creatures?" Bishop Schelker, the bishop of Bruch, stared from Gregor to Kelling and back again. "Wild animals, you mean?"

The king could only shake his head as Dr. Kelling took the decanter and poured them all a glass.

"Men," the doctor said, "or perhaps ghosts, who gathered beneath the princesses' windows to deliver a message that none of them will reveal."

"Precisely!" The word exploded from King Gregor. "The girls! Won't even speak of what happened! Shoes worn through again this morning, and Rose and Daisy both too weak to rise from their beds, yet they begged to be put back in their old rooms, and the guards removed."

King Gregor closed his eyes. "I did it, of course. How could I refuse them, with Rose so pale and worn, pleading with me like that? What am I to do, Wilhelm? Bishop? Hey? Something is not right here, not right at all."

"I agree," Schelker said quietly. "The princesses' reluctance to speak of this, even though they clearly do not enjoy their 'midnight revels' is a strong indication to me that they are doing this against their will." He clucked his tongue. "I do wish you'd told me of this sooner, Gregor."

King Gregor opened his eyes and looked down at his hands. "I didn't want you to write to the archbishop, but now I fear we must. This is surely witchcraft, and it must be stopped before my girls end up like . . ." He drew a deep breath. "Like Maude," he finished sadly.

"But consider, Gregor," Dr. Kelling said, hesitant. "If this all began with Maude, do we really want the archbishop to send someone snooping around?" The doctor bit off his words, seeing King Gregor's stricken face and Bishop Schelker's offended look. "Sorry, Schelker," Dr. Kelling murmured, contrite.

"It may surprise you, Wilhelm, but I do agree," Schelker said in his mild way. "You've known me too long to think I'm going to run straight to the archbishop at the first hint of something . . . odd. This is something best looked into by those of us who love the princesses."

"But how? What do I do?" The king's downcast eyes fell on

a letter on his desk. "Luis of Spania is sending his eldest son here on a state visit," he murmured. "I'll have to write to tell him not to come. I'll say it's because of the girls' illness."

Dr. Kelling squinted at the letter. "Gregor, a moment. Perhaps you *should* seek outside help for this dilemma."

The king stopped in the act of reaching for a blank sheet of paper. "Whose, then?"

Bishop Schelker raised his eyebrows, intrigued.

The doctor leaned back in his chair. "What if you *didn't* cancel the Spanian prince's visit?"

"What are you getting at?"

"Let him come. It's Rose I'm mostly worried about. Let this prince come, and see if he can't find out where the princesses go at night. If he does, he can . . . he can marry one of them."

King Gregor spluttered, "My daughters are not . . . *prizes* to be won in some bizarre contest!"

Dr. Kelling raised one shaggy eyebrow. "Come now! You know that the only reason Spania is sending this prince is in the hope that he'll take a fancy to one of your girls. They're waiting to see how much dowry you offer; you're waiting to see what trade agreements they'll sign. You might as well give the boy something to do while you and his father work things out."

Schelker gave a small, appreciative laugh, and looked to the king for his reaction.

King Gregor's face went red. "But, but, but the scandal! What do we do if these strange doings drive him away? I won't have my girls hurt, rejected by some Spanian fool."

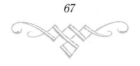

"Pish-tosh!" Dr. Kelling made a dismissive gesture. "If a bit of mystery doesn't make the girls all the more alluring, I'll eat my hat. And we don't know that the boy's a fool: by all accounts he's quite dashing. I'll send him away myself if it doesn't work. He won't want his name linked to any scandal; odds are he won't breathe a word of what's going on, just to avoid being implicated. I'll make sure to reinforce that idea when—*if*—we need to bid him farewell."

Schelker was nodding. "Think on it, Gregor. Your daughters deserve husbands who can stand up to a little intrigue, face up to these 'strange doings,' as you put it. It will be a good indication of a young man's character, to see how he reacts to this."

King Gregor sat across from his old friends for a long time, turning over the conversation in his head. "What do we tell him?"

"Tell him the girls sneak out to go dancing every night, as though it were a lark," Kelling said. "No mention of witchcraft and monsters in the garden. If he can find out where they go, he proves himself to be a resourceful candidate for the throne."

"The throne!" King Gregor's face reddened. "Now I'm to give my throne to some foreign prince?"

"Gregor," Bishop Schelker said patiently. "You have no sons, no nephews. You've always said that one of the girls' husbands would inherit. Make this a condition of that inheritance. It will be a worthy king indeed who can solve this puzzle."

King Gregor nodded slowly. "It would be a good way to find a successor. And put an end to the girls' troubles."

"You will let the Spanian prince come?" Kelling sat forward in his seat.

"I will."

Spania

Galen learned about the Spanian prince's assignment from Princess Poppy. Strong-willed Poppy had been the first of the princesses to recover her full strength, and she began to take walks in the gardens again a few days after Rionin and his shadowy companions had invaded the grounds.

She immediately sought out Galen.

"So, you're the new under-gardener," she said when she found him wrapping strips of burlap around the trunk of a weeping cherry tree. "Galen."

He straightened and bowed. "Indeed I am, Your Highness. Is there anything I can do for you?"

She peered up at him from beneath her fur-lined hood. Winter was settling in, and she had been bundled up until she could hardly move. As she studied Galen, she unwound no less than two scarves and tossed them onto a nearby bench.

"They itch," she explained. "Were you really a soldier?"

"Yes. Your Highness." Galen did not want to talk about

the war with this young girl, and he glanced down at the "tree bandages," trying to hint that he needed to keep working, without being rude.

"And did you really face off against Ri—the . . . people . . . who came into the garden the other night, with just a switch?"

"Yes, although the switches were Walter Vogel's idea. He was there with me." He thought it interesting that Poppy was more curious than afraid of what had happened that night. Both Rose and the other princess—Walter had told him it was the second eldest, Lily, who had fired the pistol—had been quite terrified.

"Walter is a dear, but quite strange," Poppy said. "I'm hardly surprised. What did you think of the creatures?"

"I—I don't really know, Your Highness. They were quite . . . I've never seen anything like them. I thought they were human, but then they seemed to just fade away."

She pounced on his description. "As if they weren't really here? As if they were an illusion?" Her expression was eager, and almost . . . hopeful.

"They weren't an illusion," Galen said. "The switches made contact; I drew blood from one I struck in the face. And the one who tried to climb the ivy, to get to your windows, certainly felt the switch on his back. It tore his coat, and I thought . . ." He stopped. For all her avid expression, she was still very young, and he didn't want to scare her.

"What did you think?"

"I thought the wounds were smoking, Your Highness." He watched her carefully.

If anything, Poppy looked disappointed. "So they really can come here," she said in a low voice.

Galen looked down at her face. There were dark circles under her eyes, and her cheeks were pale despite the cold that he knew was making his nose red under his tan. His uncle discouraged any contact between the under-gardeners and the royal family, but Reiner was on the far side of the gardens, working in the hothouses.

"Princess Poppy," Galen said, casting aside the burlap strips and taking a step toward her. "What were they? Why did they come here?"

She looked up at him with her deep blue eyes. They were violet, really, and dark with an emotion he would not have suspected her capable of, from the teasing way she had spoken before.

"They came to give us a warning," she said.

"What warning?"

"That we are not free." She gave a bitter laugh, sounding much older than her years. "And what are they? They are the things that you find crawling under a rock. Under a *stone*, actually." Again the laugh, and she started to turn away. "I should go back before someone comes after me. We are expecting a very special guest for dinner." The teasing tone was back, and she fluttered her eyelashes at Galen. "Prince Fernand of Spania! Are we not honored?"

"I'm sure he's very handsome," Galen said, managing a smile. He was still troubled by what she had said, about them not being free. And what did she mean that the invaders were things you find "under a stone"?

"But is he intelligent? That's the real question," Poppy said. "Intelligent enough to find out all our secrets? If he is, he gets to marry one of us, you know. And be the king after Papa dies."

Galen was almost more taken aback by this than by what she had said before. "What's this?"

"Father just told us," Poppy said. Her voice was still light, but Galen detected an underlying edge to it. "If Fernand can find out why our dancing shoes are worn through at night—it's now every night that it happens, you know—then he gets to pick one of us to marry, and he'll be king one day."

"And if he doesn't find out?"

"Then Papa will invite another prince, and another, until one of them does!" Her voice sounded slightly hysterical now, and she laughed, but Galen saw tears in her violet-blue eyes.

"Your Highness," he began helplessly. Then he just shook his head. Who was he to tell her it would be all right? He couldn't even begin to fathom what her life was like. Galen just took her arm and led her through the garden.

"Galen!" Uncle Reiner came out of the rose hothouse just as they were passing and stopped short when he saw who was with his nephew. He bowed. "Your Highness, please forgive young Galen's forwardness." He glared furiously over her head at Galen.

"Herr Orm," Poppy said, nodding her head at him. "Your

nephew is helping me back to the palace. I am not as well as I thought."

Reiner Orm made a harrumphing noise through his mustache but didn't say anything. He bowed again to Poppy, and Galen and the young princess strolled away.

"I think he's angry with me," Galen said out of the corner of his mouth.

"But he can't do anything about it," Poppy pointed out. "I *am* a princess, after all."

"And I'm very privileged to be able to assist you, Your Highness," Galen said with a smile.

Poppy laughed. "Rose will be jealous, if she sees us," Poppy said, looking up at Galen from under her eyelashes. "She thinks you're handsome."

Galen stopped in his tracks. Now his cheeks really were red under his tan. "But we've never . . . I only . . . by the fountain."

"She sits by the window in the afternoons, to try to get some sun. She watches you working," Poppy told him. "And she said you looked so strong and brave, standing in the moonlight with your switch that night." She giggled at Galen's discomfiture.

He gave a wary look. She was teasing him, he knew, but teasing him with the truth? Did Princess Rose watch him? He glanced up at the windows of the palace, but the angle of the weak wintry sun made it hard to tell if anyone was beyond the glass.

"Of course, she'll kill me for telling you that," Poppy said cheerfully.

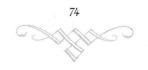

"I certainly won't tell her," Galen said fervently.

"I didn't think you would." She laughed again. "Oh, look, Prince Fernand is here." She made a face.

Someone was throwing open windows along the east side of the palace, not far from the princesses' rooms. Galen and Poppy could clearly hear orders being shouted in Spanian, and see servants running to and fro.

"Well, he sounds pleasant," Poppy said dryly.

"I'm sure he has many fine . . . qualities," Galen said.

He wasn't sure how he felt about this Spanian prince, really. Spania had been an ally of Westfalin during the war, and Galen had fought alongside some Spanian regiments. He hadn't much cared for them: they were too concerned with keeping their uniforms clean. The Westfalians tended to be a rather rough-and-tumble people. Galen wondered how a Spanian prince would like ruling over such a nation.

He saw Poppy to the wide terrace doors that faced out on the gardens. A maid scurried out immediately to scold the young girl and sweep her inside. Galen felt abashed for a moment, hoping that the maid, too, wouldn't think him forward for strolling with a princess. But instead she thanked him for finding her errant charge and returning her. Galen went back to work relieved on that count, but not on his concerns about the prince.

And the contest to win one of the princesses' hands.

Galen need not have worried about that. A week later the Spanian prince left empty-handed and furious. One of the other gardeners, who was courting a chambermaid, told Galen

and Walter that the prince had spent several nights in the hall outside the princesses' rooms, one night waiting in the garden under their windows, and had even been permitted to spend a night in the sitting room that led to their bedchambers. He had seen and heard nothing, yet their shoes were worn out every morning and they were as tired as ever.

Galen stood with Walter and watched Fernand leave. The prince was quite a dandy, and as he supervised the loading of his many trunks into the luggage wagon, he waved his arms in the air expressively and ranted to the Spanian ambassador, who had come to see him off. The lace on Fernand's cuffs flew, but his elegantly styled hair was so thickly pomaded that it hardly moved as he raged.

"Too proud," Walter commented.

"What's that?" Galen jumped. They had been standing there in silence so long that he'd almost forgotten Walter's presence.

"That young man is far too proud. He was in the gardens a few days ago, and I thought to give him some advice, the benefit of my wisdom, as it were. But he was too proud to listen."

"I see," Galen said, giving Walter a sidelong look. "And what advice did you try to give him?"

"The advice I would have given him is vastly different from that I'd have given you, young Galen," Walter said cryptically. "He hasn't been as ... blessed ... as you have been." And with that, the older man stumped away.

Shaking his head, Galen turned his attention back to the courtyard.

Seeing Galen watching him, the prince whirled around and began to rave in his direction. Galen thought about answering back, but the only Spanian he knew was extremely unflattering, so he merely bowed and went back to the gardens.

A week later, the second son of the king of La Belge arrived.

La Belge

The second son of the king of La Belge was handsome enough, Rose thought as he bowed, if you liked dark hair and blue eyes. Which Jonquil did, judging by the look on her face. As for Rose, she was indifferent, reclining on a sofa in their sitting room, propped up by pillows and draped in shawls. She nodded her head graciously.

"I am Prince Bastien," he said in heavily accented Westfalian. "It is a pleasure to meet you. All of you." His eyes flickered appraisingly over the rest of the girls.

Pansy and Petunia shared a sofa to Rose's right; Daisy was on the sofa to her left, with her twin, Poppy, curled up at her feet. None of them were at their best: red noses and watery eyes still abounded. Half of them were racked with lingering coughs, and Rose was too weak to stand for long. But her fever had cooled, so she had agreed to greet the Belgique prince formally.

"It is a pleasure to meet you, Prince Bastien," Rose said, very softly. If she talked any louder, she would cough.

Jonquil, who had recovered almost as fast as Poppy had, came to the rescue and introduced her sisters. Rose could see the prince's eyes glaze over as Jonquil rattled off the twelve flower names to him, and suppressed a sigh. From experience she knew that he would remember her name, since she was the oldest, but she steeled herself for Poppy's complaints about being called Daisy, or worse: Pansy. Few visitors could tell the twins apart, and fewer still bothered to sort out the names of anyone younger than fifteen-year-old Hyacinth.

True to form, Prince Bastien barely spared a moment on the younger girls after the introductions were made. He pulled a chair up to Rose's sofa and proceeded to regale her with the story of his journey from La Belge to Bruch. He was quite comical in his descriptions of his riverboat's captain, who spit after every sentence. Rose noticed that he didn't focus entirely on her, though, also including Jonquil and Lily in his conversation.

Later, as they dressed for dinner, Lily wryly agreed. "Oh, yes, he has his heart set on Father's throne all right. He's flirting with all three of us equally."

"Why is that?" Jonquil fussed with her hair, trying the effect of a scarlet ribbon threaded through her brunette curls. "In case one of us proves to be stupider than the others?"

"In case one of us forms a *tendre* for him and tells him the secret, is my guess," Rose said. She blew her nose into a handkerchief, relieved to be alone among her sisters where she could do so without looking unladylike. "Why did I get out of bed?"

Rose's head had been spinning by the time Prince Bastien had finished his narrative, and the effort of holding in a fit of coughing was making her breath come in gasps. One of their maids, seeing the eldest princess's distress, showed Bastien out and then hastened to get Rose out of her tea gown and into bed.

She had hoped to be able to attend the state dinner that night but sent a maid to inform her father that Lily would once more be playing hostess. She decided that Petunia, Pansy, and Daisy should stay in bed as well.

"The bow looks better at the back," she told Jonquil. "Now stop primping."

"Going to lecture me on vanity, like Hya?" Jonquil arched an eyebrow at Rose in the mirror.

"I don't care if you're vain, but you're bothering me with your rustling and humming."

"I'm not humming!"

"You are, too. You always hum when you do your hair. It's annoying."

"She's right, you know," Lily said as she put on a pair of amethyst earrings. "You hum when you do your hair, and just before you fall asleep."

Stunned by the knowledge that she had a bad habit, Jonquil finished her hair in silence and went out of the room. Rose had just closed her eyes and was starting to drift off

when she heard her younger sisters squealing and chattering in the sitting room.

Iris burst in, a huge bouquet in her hands. "Aren't they beautiful?"

She spread out the flowers, and Rose realized that there was not one large bouquet, but three small ones. One was all lilies, another all miniature irises, and the third was a cluster of deep scarlet roses.

Oddly enough, each bundle was tied with a knitted cord of black wool, but Rose thought it was quite a pretty effect as Iris handed her the scarlet roses. She held the flowers to her stuffy nose and tried to breathe in some of the scent. Only the faintest trickle of the flowers' perfume came through, so she gently stroked her cheek with the soft petals instead, savoring the exquisite feeling. She sometimes felt guilty that her father spent so much money on the gardens, especially on heating and watering the hothouses, but right now it all seemed worth it.

"Greta told me the new under-gardener brought them," Iris burbled. "He gave them to her in a big basket, and asked her to bring them to us as a special treat. I'm going to put a ribbon to match my gown around mine, and carry it at dinner." She went out, still admiring the deep purple and gold flowers of her bouquet.

"The new under-gardener?" Lily looked over her own white flowers at Rose. "Isn't he the one who made you fall in the fountain?"

"It wasn't his fault," Rose said staunchly. She had blamed Galen rather a lot in the first week of her illness, but she had felt

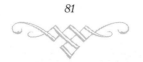

more charitable toward him recently, watching him work so tirelessly in her mother's garden. Holding the beautiful flowers to her cheek helped soothe her mood a great deal as well.

Poppy, her bouquet of bright red blooms showing up wildly against the pale pink gown she wore, stepped into the room next. "Lily, it's time for dinner. I could only just hear the gong over the sound of them gabbling out there." She jerked her dark head toward the sound of their other sisters, who were in the sitting room comparing bouquets.

"Just let me put a nicer ribbon on mine," Lily said, hurrying to her dressing table to find something to match her gown. "Why do you think he sent them? Do you suppose he got permission first?"

"I'm sure he did," Poppy said airily. "He escorted me back from the garden the other day, when Fernand arrived. He's very kind. And handsome." She wiggled her eyebrows at Rose, who chose to ignore her. "Don't get a new ribbon; they look more interesting this way," she told Lily, adjusting the cord twisted around the slim stems of her namesake. "Galen made the cord, too, I think. He sits on the rocks just beneath our windows to eat his lunch and knit. I think he knits his own socks."

"He does?" Lily looked up from the dressing table.

"Yes, but Rose would know better than I," she said mischievously. And she wandered out with her nose in her flowers.

Lily looked at Rose, who just shrugged, hoping she wasn't blushing. "He's an odd young man," she said.

"But handsome," Poppy shouted through the door.

Her two older sisters rolled their eyes.

After those who were well enough had gone to dinner, Rose closed her eyes and took a nap. She slept better than she had in weeks, months even, with the bouquet of roses propped up on the pillows near her cheek. Like Poppy, she liked the little knitted cord that held the flowers together, fingering it as she drifted off.

When she woke, Prince Bastien was leaning into her bedroom, leering at her. Startled, she clutched at the bouquet too hard, and pricked her finger on a thorn. Most of them had been stripped away, but Galen had missed one.

"Ouch!" Rose sucked at her finger, then sneezed into a handkerchief.

"Oh, poor princess," Prince Bastien said from the doorway. "You are still the sick?"

"Yes, I am still the sick," Rose retorted, irritated. She blew her nose, hard, not caring if it wasn't attractive or ladylike. She was in her nightgown; what was he doing leaning into her bedroom and staring at her like that?

"Prince Bastien?" The ever-conscientious Lily appeared at his elbow, an apologetic look in her eyes for Rose's benefit. "Why don't you show us that card game you spoke of at dinner?"

"Will not the Rose join us?"

"No, I'm afraid the Ro—my older sister is too tired," Lily said.

Lily artfully guided Prince Bastien away, and Rose spent the remainder of the evening listening to the merriment through

the open door of her bedroom. At ten o'clock, their maids readied them all for bed and prepared a cot for Prince Bastien in the sitting room. At a quarter to eleven, the maids and the Belgique prince were all fast asleep.

They would not wake until dawn, no matter what sounds the girls made. The hounds of Hell could run baying through the sitting room, but the sleep that had come over Bastien and the servants could not be disturbed.

Leaning on Lily's arm, Rose looked down at Prince Bastien as she passed him. With his mouth hanging open and a line of drool trickling onto the satin pillow, he was not as handsome as she had thought earlier. She shook her head and sniffed her flowers as Lily opened the secret passage and they went to the Midnight Ball.

Three days later, Prince Bastien left in disgust.

Hothouse

I'm not sure how many more princes they can find," Walter said. He and Galen were in the tropical hothouse, pruning exotic fruit trees that were too delicate to grow outside in Westfalin during any season. "We've gone through, what, six now?"

"Seven," Galen said.

He had been keeping careful count. Poppy, and some of the younger princesses who were feeling better, had occasionally stopped in the gardens to whisper their unflattering opinions of the princes to Galen. Rose had not come out, though Galen often saw her at the windows. She looked so pale, with her golden-brown hair crowning her wan face. He had wanted to send more bouquets, but there were rather too many princesses for such a thing to go unnoticed, and it wouldn't be proper for Galen to be sending flowers to Rose alone. He had excused his first gift by saying that they were the flowers from the hothouse that needed to be thinned out anyway.

"And every one of them arrogant and self-serving," Walter

said, clucking his tongue. "Without a care for the princesses beyond getting the throne."

And all seven had left without solving the mystery of the worn-out dancing slippers. The king could be heard shouting at all hours of the day and night to anyone who would listen. Relations were even more strained with their neighbor nations than they had been before. If King Gregor had thought that a contest to win his throne would bring the countries of Ionia closer together, he had been wrong.

"It's been three months," Galen said suddenly.

Walter just grunted.

"Princess Rose has been ill for three months."

"She's on the mend," Walter assured him. "Pneumonia is never easy, even on the young." Walter patted Galen's arm. "You're a good lad to worry about them, Galen. A very good lad."

Just then the door at the far end of the hothouse opened, and a pair of figures came through. They were heavily bundled against the cold, and all Galen could say for sure was that they were female. The two figures divested themselves of their bonnets and cloaks, steaming in the sudden heat, and Galen saw that it was Princess Rose herself, leaning on the arm of the musically inclined princess—Violet, he thought her name was.

Violet helped Rose to a little bench beneath a banana tree, and then wandered off to look at some flowering vines. Galen put down his pruning shears. Walter raised an eyebrow, and Galen grinned. He picked an orange from a nearby tree, winked at Walter, and strolled down the aisle to the bench.

Now that he had spent more time working around the palace, running into princesses and ministers of state, ambassadors, and the occasional prince, his manners were much more refined. "Good morning, Princess Rose," he said gallantly, and offered her the orange with a flourish.

In truth, he was a little shocked by her appearance. At her window she appeared romantically pale and slender, but up close she was too thin and hollow cheeked, with dark circles under her eyes. Her thick golden-brown hair was pulled back tightly in a simple braid, which emphasized the taut whiteness of her skin against the dark-colored dress she wore.

Still, Galen did not let his smile slip. She was even more beautiful now, he thought, with an otherworldly quality to her and a maturity that had not been there before.

"Allow me to give you this orange, Your Highness, along with my wishes for a swift recovery."

"That's very generous of you, Master Galen," she replied, a faint light kindling in her eyes, "especially since they are my family's oranges." She took it from him, rolling it between her palms. "And considering that my illness is most likely a result of falling into the fountain the day we met."

Galen winced. He had known she would remember that, but he had hoped she wouldn't hold it against him. Although, judging by the faint smile on her pale lips, she didn't mean it in earnest.

"Well, Your Highness, I know that I am indeed handsome, but I can hardly be blamed if my good looks overcame you so strongly that you fainted," he said, striking a pose. He had

butterflies in his stomach, wondering if he was taking the teasing too far.

But he was rewarded: Rose laughed, a high, clear sound, and lobbed the orange at him. He caught it deftly, but when her laughter turned to a cough, he dropped the orange and bent over her, not sure if he dared to pat her back or take her hand. "Your Highness, forgive me. Are you unwell?"

Violet heard the coughing and came running back. She sank down on the bench beside Rose, putting her arm around the older girl and holding a handkerchief to Rose's lips. "What happened?" she asked Galen, her tone just shy of being accusatory.

"I am so sorry, Your Highness," Galen said, backing away. "I made her laugh, and—"

"You made her laugh?" Violet's eyes widened. "She hasn't laughed in weeks!" She smiled at Galen and gave Rose's shoulders a little squeeze.

"Oh, dear," Rose gasped, her coughing finished. "I'm sorry," she said to Galen.

"No, please, Your Highness, the fault was all mine." He cleared his throat. "Did you . . . did you like the bouquet? The bouquets, I mean? A month or so ago? I sent . . ." He trailed off, feeling foolish.

"Oh, yes!" Rose smiled warmly at him. "They were beautiful."

"I still have mine," Violet piped up. "I dried it, and it's in a little vase on my pianoforte."

"I'm glad," Galen told her, but his eyes were on Rose. "I

hoped that you would like them." Rose thought the bouquet he made for her had been beautiful.

"Oh, that reminds me." Rose fished in the pocket of her cloak and brought out the cord Galen had used to tie her bouquet. "Would you like this back? I'm sure it will come in handy."

"No, no! You must keep it, Princess Rose," Galen said. "The old soldier who taught me how to knit always said that a knitted cord made with black wool can ward off evil. I thought perhaps—" He stopped, embarrassed. He had given them the bouquets wrapped with black wool cord to stave off their illness, but he knew that it was not his place.

"Well, thank you," Rose said, apparently not noticing his hesitation. She coiled the little cord and put it back in her pocket.

Then there was nothing else to say, and Galen stood before the two princesses, looking awkward. "Well." He rocked on his heels, thinking that he had better get back to work before Reiner came by and berated him. "Since I'm sure you are enjoying the many royal suitors who have come to gaze upon your beauty, I suppose I had better take myself off." He bowed. "I would hate to be challenged to a duel."

Galen grinned and winked as he said this, but was shocked by their responses. Rose closed her eyes and looked pained, and Violet actually crossed herself and muttered a prayer.

There was a noise behind him, and Galen turned to see two of the middle princesses, with the youngest in tow. They were all staring at him with appalled expressions.

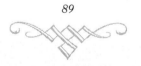

"Is he talking about the princes who died?" Petunia asked. She frowned at Galen. "We're not supposed to talk about them," she said in a loud whisper.

"Who . . . died?" Galen's voice faltered.

"Ssshh!" Petunia was dragged away by the two sisters holding her hands. "Sssssh!" she said over her shoulder, still glaring at Galen.

"Rose, we should go back to our rooms. You should rest," Violet said stiffly, not meeting Galen's eyes. Only moments before she had been beaming at him for making her eldest sister smile. Galen's heart sank.

"No," Rose said, shaking her off. "He has a right to know. Everyone does."

"But, Rose," Violet protested. "He's a *gardener*. He doesn't have anything to do with this."

Anger flashed through Galen, and he fought it down. "She's right," Galen said, turning away. "I'm just a gardener." He didn't want to cause Rose any more embarrassment.

"They say you were once a soldier," Rose called after him. "That you fought in the war."

He turned back slowly, straightening his shoulders. "That is true, Your Highness."

"Then do you know the roads to the south of Westfalin, that lead to Spania and to Analousia?"

"Indeed I do, Your Highness. I traveled them, returning from the war." He thought of the strange old woman he had met on his way, and the cloak she had given him. It was hidden in the chest in his room back at his uncle's house. A cloak of invisibility was of little use to an under-gardener.

"Are there many bandits on those roads? Were you in great danger?" Rose's face was strange, as though she already knew the answer.

"No, Your Highness." Galen shook his head, puzzled. "There are few farms along those roads, but the people were kind to a weary soldier. Perhaps, since I returned, things have changed. But it has been only a few months. . . ."

She was already shaking her head. "Everyone says the same. There have never been thieves along those roads, or cause for concern. And yet, the Spanian prince who came courting, and tried to . . . to spy on us at night, was killed by brigands on his way home."

Galen drew back. "I am very sorry, Your Highnesses." He recalled the foppish prince he had seen screeching at the porters in the courtyard. The prince's sword had looked mostly ornamental and probably would not have deterred a professional highwayman. "But he had guards to . . ." Seeing their distressed faces, he stopped speculating. "I'm sorry that you are grieved at the loss of your friend, Your Highnesses."

Rose waved this aside. "He was hardly our friend," she said, absently digging the toe of her low boot into the soft earth around the bench. "Neither were the princes of La Belge and Analousia. Otherwise we would be prostrate with grief, for they are dead too."

"What's this?" Galen had come all the way back, and now

stood directly before the two young women. Realizing that his jaw was hanging open, he shut it with a click.

"They dueled," Violet said shortly. "They met at the Belgique court a week after the Analousian prince failed. He accused the Belgique prince—I cannot remember their names, forgive me—of sabotage, claiming that the Belgique prince had left traps here, to ensure that the Analousian prince would fail and be humiliated. It wasn't true, but they fought, and killed each other."

Speechless, Galen only stared at her.

"The others are dead as well," Rose added. "All the princes who have come here have died. A ship sank. A normally gentle horse spooked and threw his rider, breaking the poor prince's neck." She looked up at Galen. "We are cursed. That is why you deserve to know: our family is cursed. You should leave; find work elsewhere before something happens to you, too."

Galen rallied. "But, Princess Rose! You aren't cursed. You've been ill, but surely that—"

She cut him off with a sharp gesture of her hand and got to her feet with an effort. "We are cursed," she said with finality. As she passed him, leaning on Violet's arm, she touched Galen's shoulder with a thin hand. "Leave this place," she said softly.

When Uncle Reiner found him some minutes later, Galen was still standing in the middle of the walkway. He was thinking furiously, staring at the bench where Rose and Violet had been sitting.

"Galen! Don't you have any work to do?" Reiner looked

like he could easily find some for the young man, if he was at a loss. "And why is there an orange lying on the ground?"

Galen looked up at him. "I'm going to solve the puzzle," he said.

"What are you babbling about?" Reiner held out a trowel and a packet of seeds, but Galen didn't take them.

"I must see the king," he muttered under his breath, pushing past Reiner and going out of the hothouse. "Poor Rose. I must help her."

Dancer

Rose's days passed in a fog.

Her pneumonia had given her a reprieve from her usual duties as hostess, and Lily or Jonquil stood in her place, depending on which of them was feeling better. Rose had always thought the state dinners and official receptions boring, but now that she did not attend them she realized how much of a diversion they had provided. Her schooling was done, and she did not have hobbies like Violet or Hyacinth did to keep her busy. She enjoyed reading, but her fever and exhaustion made it hard for her to concentrate. She had been working her way through the same Bretoner novel since the week before her illness began, and she still had not finished it.

Now that she was well enough to leave her rooms for an hour or so at a time, it was too cold to go anywhere. She didn't have friends outside the palace to visit, and the gardens were out of the question. It was Violet who had suggested the hothouse where the exotic fruits and rare orchids were grown, and had put aside her music to help Rose bundle up and walk there.

The tropical hothouse where, on a bench beneath a banana tree, she had come face-to-face with Galen again.

Rose was startled by how pleased she was to see him standing there in his brown gardening smock. After the parade of self-important princes that had gone by, since rendered faceless by her illness, she found Galen's easy manners and warm, sincere smile refreshing. He had cropped his hair again, so short that you could see his scalp along the sides. His hair was wiry, and she had the urge to rub his head and feel it.

She hadn't meant to become so morbid with Galen, to tell him that they were cursed. It was how she felt, though. And the indignity of finding that her father was offering one of them as a prize in this contest combined with the horror of hearing about the princes' deaths had added to her despair.

It was not at all reassuring to find that Hyacinth shared her fears. "You are right," she told Rose solemnly. "At first I thought we were innocent, and only Mother would be punished. But now, with the princes' deaths on our heads, I'm certain of it." She did not sound upset by this, merely resigned.

Poppy mimed silencing Hyacinth by putting a pillow over the latter's head, but Daisy pulled her twin away. Annoyed, Poppy buried her own face in the pillow. "You can all be cursed if you want," came her muffled voice, "but I prefer to think about the future."

"Which is?" Jonquil raised an eyebrow. The sisters were all in their sitting room. Some were sewing; the younger ones had

a jigsaw puzzle spread across the floor. Rose reclined on a divan by the window, tired from her walk back from the hot-house.

"Our time below will end, and we will be free," Poppy said resolutely.

"What are my princesses about this fine day?" Anne, their plump governess, came bustling into the room.

Anne was Breton born and had come to Bruch as a companion and translator for Queen Maude. When Rose turned four, Anne had been persuaded to take up the position of royal governess, since her accomplishments included speaking Analousian, playing the pianoforte, and possessing a knowledge of history and the sciences, in addition to her fluency in both Bretoner and Westfalian. She was both a friend and a teacher to the girls, and Rose bitterly regretted that they could not tell Anne about the curse.

Poppy opened her mouth to answer the governess, then closed it again, unable to speak. It was no use attempting to confide in their governess, or anyone else. Their voices would simply fade away or nonsense would come spewing out, and the princesses had long ago stopped trying.

"Nothing," Poppy muttered finally.

"Since you are well enough to talk about 'nothing,' why don't we talk about Westfalian history?" Anne looked from one sister to the other with bright black eyes. She reminded Rose of a large sparrow.

The sisters who were still schooling age all groaned as they

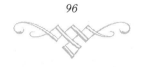

followed Anne into the schoolroom, leaving the older set behind.

"Rose, we are not cursed," Lily said. She crossed the room to her older sister and tucked an afghan around Rose's knees. "Don't dwell on it. A few more years . . ."

"A few more years, and I'll be dead," Rose retorted, turning away from Lily. She stared out at the winter garden. She could see old Walter going along the path below with a barrow full of mulch and a trio of under-gardeners following him. Her heart skipped a beat, but when she saw that none of them was Galen, it subsided. She sighed.

Lily felt her forehead. "Are you feeling worse? Should you be in bed?"

"No, I'll be fine." She summoned a smile. "Really, I just want to sit here and rest, thank you."

Rose must have fallen asleep, because the next thing she knew, Jonquil was shaking her awake. The younger girl was already dressed in a gown of pink satin, her hair done up in ribbons.

"It's half past eleven," Jonquil said, resignation in her voice. "Let's get you ready."

As they had since the first day of her illness, Lily and Jonquil helped Rose into a ball gown. They rouged her cheeks and arranged her hair, then laced on the new dancing slippers that had been delivered that day.

She was strong enough to dress herself, at this point, but

holding her arms over her head to fix her hair still made her breathless. She toyed with the idea of going to the Midnight Ball in a nightgown and bedroom slippers, to emphasize the fact that she was not well and should not be forced to attend, but made the mistake of sharing the idea with Lily.

Lily was horrified, fearing that if any one of them was not looking her best, they would all be punished. Things had been even more strained since they had missed a night, so Rose permitted them to dress her in satin and drape her with jewels. Then she looked on while the rest of her sisters, down to weeping, cough-racked Pansy, were similarly attired.

Kind-hearted Iris tucked pillows under the heads of their snoring maids and put blankets over them. Shortly after entering the princesses' apartments following dinner, they had been stricken by the sleeping charm, as always, and sank down on the floor in a deep sleep. They would awaken in the morning, stiff and groggy, to find their charges safely in bed, the brand-new dancing shoes full of holes.

"Are we ready?" Lily looked at her eleven sisters. It had always been Rose who had asked, who had checked lacings and tucked up loose curls. But since her illness, Rose had had neither the strength nor the inclination, so Lily had taken on this task as well.

They all nodded in agreement, Rose sagging between Poppy and Violet, Pansy supported by Orchid and Daisy, and Jonquil propping up Iris. Petunia, Hyacinth, and Lilac all held hands, Petunia actually smiling, for she still loved to dance. Lily knelt in the middle of the Araby rug that covered the sitting room floor. With one long finger, she traced the maze pattern at the center of the rug.

The maze shimmered. What had been gold-colored silk became gold in truth, and it spiraled down through the floor, the gleaming stripes widening into angular stairs that led into darkness. Lily took a lamp from the table and stepped delicately onto the first step, her free hand holding her skirts out of the way. One by one the sisters descended, with Rose bringing up the rear.

At the bottom of the stairs the darkness swallowed them. Once Rose had stepped onto level ground, the golden spiral ascended again, leaving them with no means of escape until the first light of dawn touched the eastern hills of Westfalin. How Rionin and his brothers had reached the king's garden, how their mother had first made contact with such creatures, they had never dared ask.

Lily's lamp was little more than a spark, and they followed it with eyes hungry for its light. Through the gate, through forest, to the shores of the lake, over the water to the Midnight Ball.

Spy

When Galen had rushed off to speak to King Gregor more than a month ago, he ran afoul of the palace's butler, Herr Fischer. Herr Fischer did not allow under-gardeners wearing muddy smocks to speak to the king. Herr Fischer did not allow under-gardeners into the palace at all.

But as Galen was turning away, dejected, he had passed Dr. Kelling arriving at the palace to check on the princesses. Dr. Kelling hailed Galen, curious about the young man's forlorn expression as he trudged away from the front doors.

"Hello there! May I be of assistance?"

Galen had seen the doctor coming and going in the past, and knew that he was a close friend of the royal family. The physician had an unruly mop of gray hair and impressive eyebrows over twinkling blue eyes.

"Yes, Herr Doctor," Galen said. "I had hoped . . . well, I had hoped to speak to the king." Galen gritted his teeth, realizing how foolish he sounded. What right had he to speak to the king?

"Concerning what? Is there a problem with the Queen's Garden?"

"Oh, no, sir," Galen assured him. "It's was about . . . about the princesses. I thought that I might be able to . . . help." Galen squared his shoulders and looked Dr. Kelling in the eyes. Perhaps he was getting above himself, but he couldn't bear to see Rose so exhausted and bitter. "I want to help them, sir," Galen said firmly.

"What makes you think the princesses need help?" One of the impressive eyebrows was raised.

Galen looked at him. Looked down at him, actually. Dr. Kelling was of average height, which meant that Galen topped him by nearly a head.

"Sir, everyone knows about the worn-out dancing slippers and the princesses being so exhausted all the time. They've been sick. It can't help that they go . . . wherever it is they go every night." He grimaced. "And I saw the . . . people or whatever they were, that came into the garden the night after they didn't dance."

Dr. Kelling gave Galen an appraising look. "What is it you think you can do?"

Galen stopped walking. He had already decided that telling people he had a cloak that rendered him invisible was danger-ous. He could be accused of witchcraft, or simply of being mad if no one believed him. He'd come up with a plausible lie, and he would ask God for forgiveness later.

"I learned things in the army, sir," Galen said. "Scouting, spying, that sort of thing. I am sure that I can observe the princesses without them knowing."

Kelling nodded slowly, and started walking back to the palace. "You were a soldier?"

"Yes, sir."

"You barely look old enough to have seen the last battle."

"My father was a career army man, sir. I was there at the first engagement with Analousia, and took up my father's rifle when I was barely fifteen."

"Saints preserve us," Dr. Kelling said, and squeezed Galen's shoulder. "What have we done to our youth?" His bright eyes studied Galen's tanned face and he shook his head. "What's your name, lad?"

"Galen Werner, sir."

"Well, Galen Werner, perhaps a talented spy *is* what we need, instead of these princes stumbling about in the dark. First, I must see to my patients, but after that I will be taking lunch with His Majesty and I shall speak to him about your idea. In the meantime you'd better continue with your work. I know Reiner Orm, and he will not be pleased if he catches you hanging about the front drive."

"No, sir," Galen said with a smile.

He loped off, hope rising in his chest. Dr. Kelling would speak to the king and Galen would get permission to snoop around at night. With his cloak he would be able to follow Rose and her sisters and discover what madness had caught them up in its web. Soon the princesses would be able to rest,

and they would get well. Smiling, he imagined the flush of health on Princess Rose's cheek. He would not be offered her hand in marriage, of course. But perhaps he might ask to dance with her at a ball, or sit with her at dinner, just once.

Whistling, he took up his rake.

He was still in good spirits when a message from the doctor was delivered by one of the footmen. Galen would not be allowed inside the palace, but he would be permitted to roam the gardens all night. If he had anything to report, Galen was to leave a message with one of the indoor staff, addressed to either King Gregor or Dr. Kelling. There was a letter with the king's seal included, giving him the freedom of the palace grounds after the other gardeners had gone home and the gates had been locked.

Now singing under his breath, Galen continued his work until sunset and walked home with Uncle Reiner as usual. They had a fine dinner, and Galen went up to his room afterward as though nothing were out of the ordinary. Reiner Orm had a strict sense of class and propriety, and Galen knew it would be useless to tell his relations what he was about. After ten, when he was sure everyone else was asleep, Galen stuffed the dull purple cape into his satchel and slipped out of the house.

It was strange to walk the streets of Bruch at night. During the day they were all a-bustle: carts and horses, people on foot, neighbors calling out to one another. But now they were silent. A cold rain had fallen and the streets gleamed, slick and wet, in the moonlight.

Stranger still was approaching the guards at the palace gate and showing them the king's letter. Once he was well away from the gatehouse, in the shadows of a dripping oak tree, Galen pulled the cloak out of his satchel and put it on. As soon as the gold clasp was fastened, he disappeared. He hurried down the gravel paths to the south side of the palace and took up his position just below the princesses' windows.

There were some large ornamental boulders where he and Walter often sat to eat their lunch. They were cold now, and wet, so Galen didn't sit, but paced around them to keep warm while he watched the windows.

A slim form appeared, drawing aside one of the curtains to look out, and Galen's heart began to pound. Then she turned her head, and Galen realized that the profile did not belong to Rose, but Jonquil, and he laughed at himself. He should have known, seeing the towering confection of ribbons and curls on her head, that it was not Rose. Jonquil closed the curtains and moved away, and Galen continued to pace, berating himself silently.

Surely he wasn't foolish enough to fall in love with a princess. . . .

He shook his head and turned his mind instead to Jonquil's appearance. Her hair clearly had been done for a formal occasion, and it looked as if she had been wearing a ball gown and jewels. So then, they were going somewhere to dance. She would not be so elaborately dressed merely to dance in her room with her sisters.

He waited all night on the south side of the palace. The

lights never dimmed in the princesses' rooms, and though Galen stared at the filmy curtains, willing them to part so that he could see inside, no one came to the window again. Only when dawn came were the lights within snuffed out one by one.

Galen did not give up hope. According to the king's letter, he could return to the palace after hours as often as it took to uncover the secret, and he would. He would check every door and window that the princesses might possibly use, might even climb the ivy that Rionin had attempted to climb and peek in their windows, though the idea made him flush.

He also decided to confide in Walter. The aged gardener had a keen eye. Galen would set him to looking for any sign of footprints in the soft earth of the flower beds. Surely twelve pairs of feet could not pass through the garden without leaving a mark.

Breton

"Do you care for *roses*, Princess *Rose*?" Prince Alfred of Breton smiled at Rose in what he probably thought was a flirtatious manner. It revealed a great many long teeth, however, and made him look even more like a horse. Rose said a silent prayer of thanks that she didn't have teeth like that. Alfred was her second cousin on her mother's side and the possessor of a host of traits that Rose felt lucky not to have inherited.

"Yes, yes I do," Rose said, keeping her voice level. She did not find the pun on her name amusing, and refused to show any emotion that might be construed as amusement by the clueless Alfred.

They were standing in the rose hothouse, admiring the flowers that bloomed there all year long. This was Head Gardener Orm's pet project: he was breeding new colors and types of roses, something that keenly interested King Gregor as well. The bush that Rose and Prince Alfred stood before bore pink roses with scarlet centers. Each bloom was the size of a saucer.

"Then I shall pluck a rose for your hair," Prince Alfred brayed, lunging forward and snatching at one of the flowers. "Even as I shall pluck out the secret that haunts you every night!" His horsy laugh was cut short by a cry of pain as a thorn pricked him.

"Serves him right," Rose thought. The princesses all knew that these roses were not for picking, and Rose had warned Prince Alfred when they entered the hothouse. Once the blooms were almost blown, the head gardener carefully cut them and brought them to the palace to be displayed for a brief time, but otherwise they were purely for "floral experimentation," as her father called it.

Besides which, this Bretoner prince was getting on Rose's nerves. His obnoxious laughter and alarming teeth were only the half of it. He peppered his conversation with clumsily suggestive remarks, and clearly thought himself quite the gallant. Rose's sisters had all managed to flee after only a few minutes in his presence, leaving Rose to entertain Alfred on her own.

She gritted her teeth as she offered him a handkerchief, plotting the revenge she would take on her sisters for abandoning her with Prince Horseface. She told herself that the week would go by quickly enough, and then he would be sent away in disgrace like all the others. But as he bled into her clean handkerchief and complimented her tender touch, she remembered that once he was sent away, his life would likely be cut short in some mysterious accident. She should want him to succeed, but he was not remotely the dashing figure she had imagined saving her from the Midnight Balls.

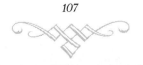

"I'm an evil person," she mumbled under her breath.

"What was that, dear, dear Rose?" Alfred wrinkled his nose at her in what she supposed was meant to be an alluring way.

"I—I—" She couldn't think of anything. She was staring at his large, slightly bulging eyes and couldn't seem to look away.

"I beg your pardon, Your Highnesses." Galen Werner stepped around some potted roses and gave them a brief bow. "Prince Alfred is wanted back at the palace."

"I am? Why?" Prince Alfred looked mystified, and Rose agreed silently: why would anyone want *him*?

"I couldn't say, Your Highness," Galen said. "I'm only an under-gardener."

Alfred struck a dramatic pose, somewhat ruined by the bloody scrap of linen clutched in one hand. "I shall be but a moment, fair princess," he whinnied.

"Very well," was all Rose could say.

After Prince Alfred had gone, Rose sank down on a small bench with a sigh. She closed her eyes and leaned her head back. Galen was still hovering nearby, looking at her with concern.

"Do you need anything, Your Highness?"

She opened her eyes and looked at him. "Why was Prince Alfred needed at the palace?"

Galen flushed. "He, well, I couldn't say. . . ."

Rose burst out laughing. "Did you just say that to get rid of him?"

"Er, yes." Galen looked around sheepishly. "He seemed to be bothering Your Highness."

"Oh, he was," she agreed, giving him a grateful smile. "And my traitorous sisters abandoned me!"

"Very cruel of them."

"Very." She gave a little shudder. "Did you see his *teeth*?"

"He does have . . . very large teeth," Galen said. "I'm sure that he has other fine features, however," Galen added, not very convincingly.

"His teeth are probably his best feature, I'm afraid," Rose said, still laughing. "I feel cruel saying such things, especially since we are related . . . but he's so vain!"

Galen looked thoughtful. "He does remind me of a very handsome cart horse I once knew," he said. "They had the same color hair."

Rose laughed aloud again. It felt good to be able to laugh without coughing, but more than that, it felt good just to find something to laugh about. That morning her father had taken her aside after breakfast and begged her to let Alfred uncover their secret.

"My dear," King Gregor had said, tears in his eyes. "I am pleading with you: let this young fool succeed. I do not know what secret you keep, or why, but it must end. Please, Rosie." He cleared his throat. "Not the man I would have picked for you, for any of you, but rumors are racing through the Ionian courts. They're saying that you poor girls must have had a hand in these unfortunate deaths. I don't know if offering my kingdom is incentive enough to draw another suitor."

Rose grieved that their curse had brought her father to this state—begging with bloodshot eyes for a foolish, horse-faced prince to win her hand—but there was nothing she could do. She could no more speak of the curse than she could prevent the enchanted sleep from overtaking Alfred that night and the nights after.

"Now, what's made you look sad?" Galen stared down at her, anxious.

She blinked away her memories of this morning. "Nothing." She shrugged. "Just the thought that if horrible Prince Alfred doesn't—" She realized that she was confiding her family's problems to one of the gardeners and stopped herself short. "It's nothing."

"You're worried that Prince Alfred, horrible as he is, will come to harm, and you'll be blamed?" Galen's voice was gentle.

Tears pricked Rose's eyes, her laughter gone. She nodded. "Father's at his wit's end."

"You can't tell anyone what's going on, can you?"

She shook her head.

"Not even me? I'm not a prince," he wheedled.

"No one," she said with a little hiccup.

Galen took out a pair of gardening shears and went to the bush with the pink-and-scarlet roses. He neatly cut the stem of the bloom Alfred had tried to pick and peeled off the thorns before offering it to Rose.

"I shouldn't," she protested.

"It's already done," he told her. "Don't let it go to waste."

Their fingers touched when she took it from him, and they stayed that way for a moment, hands together, the rose cradled between them.

Rose was just thinking of something she could say, something to break the comfortable silence that she was enjoying far too much, when she heard the hothouse door open and close. She and Galen stepped apart; he gave her a little bow and slipped away.

Prince Alfred came huffing down the path, red in the face and irritable. "No one in the palace seems to have the faintest idea what that half-witted gardener was talking about," he complained.

"Perhaps he misheard," Rose said. She was still gazing down at the perfect flower cupped in her hand.

"And on the way back, an old man with a peg leg accosted me, trying to get me to wear some smelly herb on my lapel!" Alfred blew through his wet lips. "In Breton—"

"Perhaps *I* was the one wanted back at the palace," Rose interrupted. "I'd best return." Tucking the rose into the sash of her high-waisted gown, she got up and walked past the still-blathering Prince Alfred, pulling her cloak tight around her.

That was another thing about Prince Alfred that drove Rose—and everyone else—to distraction. He never stopped talking. He talked about himself. He talked about his prize-winning hounds and his prize-winning horses. He talked about Breton, and how everything there was superior to everything in Westfalin, from the weather to the pigs. By dinner, Rose was ready to stuff her handkerchief in his mouth to silence him.

She settled for not listening. In fact, she didn't even pretend to listen. No one did. But either he didn't notice or it didn't bother him in the slightest. After dinner Alfred followed the sisters to their rooms, where he talked all through several games of cards. In fact, the enchantment caught him mid-sentence, and he went from babbling about his hounds (again) to snoring, with his cheek on the ace of spades in the space of a heartbeat.

"Whew!" Poppy threw down her cards. "What a nightmare! I wasn't sure if the magic would even work on him."

"I thought he was going to keep talking, even if he fell asleep," Orchid said.

"Now, now," Hyacinth chided them, "we should be more charitable."

"I agree with Poppy," Rose said, to everyone's surprise. "I was ready to knock him over the head with a vase if the spell didn't get him." She tossed down her own cards in disgust.

Prince Alfred's snores were particularly loud in the silence that followed Rose's outburst. They almost harmonized with the snores coming from the two maids in the other room, and a tinkling sound, like wind chimes or bells, that seemed to be coming from outside.

"What is that noise?" Daisy looked around, puzzled. "I've been hearing it all day."

"One of the gardeners put bells in the ivy outside our window," Lilac said.

"Why?"

"Why do the gardeners do anything?" Lilac shrugged.

"We might as well go now," said Rose. The bells couldn't drown out all the snoring, so what good were they?

"Why are you in such a hurry?" twelve-year-old Iris wanted to know. "You're the one who's always moaning and complaining about the Midnight Ball."

"Because I want this night to be over with," Rose snapped. "I want all these nights to be over with."

Her dislike of Prince Alfred had given her a hectic energy. She knelt on the carpet and stroked the pattern, opening the door into the world below. She took a lamp and started down, not looking back to see if her sisters followed.

Shawl

Prince Alfred came and Prince Alfred went, just like all the others. Within a week of his return to Breton, he was trampled by one of his prize horses and killed.

King Gregor sent gifts for the royal family and a letter expressing his deepest regrets. The Bretoner king responded by sending the letter and gifts back, unopened, along with the Westfalin ambassador, who was no longer welcome at the royal court in Castleraugh.

"Sire! This is an outrage! A blatant slap in the face!" Lord Schilling, the prime minister, was scarlet with rage. "It's practically a declaration of war—"

"No!" Now it was King Gregor's turn to grow red and shout. "No more war! We swallow the insult and move on. The poor man's grief-stricken. He lost his eldest son and he lashed out; I can understand that."

King Gregor was in the council chamber with his ministers, talking over the snub from Breton. Rose sat in one corner, quietly hemming handkerchiefs. One of the girls always sat in on royal councils, as their mother had done, to offer the king silent support.

"But, sire," the prime minister protested, "my spies in Analousia say that there have been meetings between their prime minister and the Belgique ambassador. And Spanian relations are frigid at best now." He clenched his fists and barreled on. "They are saying that these princes are not dying by accident, that these are very cleverly arranged assassinations. Your Majesty, they are pointing the blame squarely at you. Our foreign relations are in a worse state now than they were during the war! What are we to do?"

The hush that followed Schilling's words was profound. Rose dropped her sewing, and the small ping of her needle hitting the polished wood floor was far too loud. The prime minister looked at her with hard eyes.

"We are to ignore it," King Gregor said, voice grim. "I don't care if we do look like fools: we will continue to smile and seek peace while they mutter and rattle their swords. It is all we can do. This country will not survive another war."

Rose shuddered. She and her sisters knew full well what price had been paid to ensure that Westfalin would win the Analousian war. If another war came . . . she could not imagine what would become of their poor country then. She dared not make the bargains her mother had made. Westfalin would have to rise or fall on its own strength, and right now that strength was not great.

"Then at least rescind that ridiculous proclamation," the

prime minister was pleading now. "No more princes will be coming. Don't flaunt the fact that every royal house in Ionia has lost a prince because of your daughters."

There was a collective gasp from the other councillors.

"You go too far," King Gregor said in a low voice. "My daughters are innocent. These deaths . . . are terrible. . . ." He rubbed his mouth with one hand as though washing away a bad taste. "But how can anyone say it's Lily's fault when a horse in Polen throws its rider? Or little Petunia's idea for two young hotheads to duel?"

With a sick heart, Rose noticed that her father would not even look in her direction when he said this.

Schilling chewed his mustache, clearly biting back a retort. When at last he spoke, his voice was barely under control. "Paying the discharge wages for the army nearly bankrupted us. Now relations with both our former enemies and our allies are strained to breaking point. If we are accused, directly, of having their sons killed . . . If the archbishop hears these rumors, rumors that we are causing these accidents from hundreds of miles away . . ."

There was another silence after that, for not even Schilling knew what else to say.

Rose sat, clutching her sewing in clammy hands. She felt like the floor was falling away beneath her chair and had to struggle to breathe evenly and not let her distress attract attention.

Before the silence became truly unbearable, Rose's father simply repeated his orders for everyone to "hold firm," and the council was dismissed.

Rose tucked her snarled thread into her sewing basket and stood up.

"Rosie?" Her father gave her a look that was equal parts hopeful and angry.

She knew what he wanted: he wanted her to tell him their secret. Or at least, to tell him it was all over with, that the sleepless nights—on everyone's part—were done. He had talked at breakfast of sending the younger set to the old fortress in the mountains, and Rose had had to tell him that the shadowy figures in the garden would return, and that this time they might enter the palace itself. She couldn't say any more, but the expression on her face and the faces of her sisters had been enough to convince him to let them be.

She gave him a tight smile and slipped out of the room. She stopped in her own rooms only long enough to drop her sewing basket on a chair and put a long fur-lined cloak over her wool gown before setting out for the gardens.

In the hothouse with the experimental roses, she ran into Head Gardener Orm. He gave her a grim nod as he carefully inspected the leaves of the pink-and-scarlet rosebush. She tried not to look too guilty, certain that he knew about Galen cutting one of the flowers for her, and backed out.

She wandered, disconsolate, into the other hothouses, but couldn't find Galen. She wasn't even sure why she was looking for him, but she was sick to death of her sisters, and there was no one else near her age in the palace. Anne, their governess, had always been the girls' confidant, but it was lesson time. And even had Anne been free, Rose did not feel the

need to seek her out as strongly as she longed to speak with Galen.

"Rose! Rose! Rose!"

The younger set came tumbling across the winter-brown lawns to meet her. They were red-cheeked from the cold, their hair and cloaks flying. Rose judged that they had just been released from their lessons for the day.

"Rosie-rosie-rose-rose," sang Orchid. "You have a present!"

"*I* want a present too," Pansy said, pouting. "Where's *my* present?"

"It is not your birthday," Petunia said with great authority. "There are only presents on your birthday and the holidays."

"But it's not Rose's birthday either," Orchid said, dancing around Rose. "That's what makes it an extra-special present."

All the dancing and pouting and singing, after her long walk across the gardens and back, was making Rose tired. She took hold of Pansy with one hand and Orchid with the other and continued walking back to the palace. Petunia followed obediently.

"Now," said Rose when they had calmed down. "What's this about a present?"

The younger set could only babble that one of the maids had been given the present by a tall young man who said it was for Rose. When they reached the princesses' apartments, Poppy filled in the details.

"One of the under-gardeners sent you a present," she said, her eyes sparkling with mischief. "I think you can guess which one, can't you?" She shook back her dark hair. "No guesses?

Well, it was the handsome one. The young, handsome one with the broad shoulders. The one who *fancies* you. What's his name again? Oh, yes! Galen!"

Her twin, Daisy, frowned. "He doesn't fancy Rose," she said earnestly. "It's impossible: he's a commoner."

Rose brushed aside that remark.

"What about Heinrich and Lily?" Poppy's eyes sparked with challenge.

"May I see my present?" Rose interrupted, not wanting to stir up old heartaches even though Lily wasn't there. Thinking of the handsome young soldier—so like Galen in appearance—gave her a pang. She knew Lily still grieved for him. Rose gave a significant look to the package, neatly wrapped in brown paper, that Poppy was holding.

The younger girl handed it over, and Rose took it to her favorite divan by the window. Her sisters followed her. Rose gave them another look. The younger set didn't understand, but Poppy did. With a sigh, she pulled them away, taking her twin with her. They sat on the other side of the sitting room, watching Rose.

Realizing that was as much privacy as she was going to get, Rose turned her attention to the package. It was lightweight and soft within the crackling paper. It had been tied with yarn rather than string, pretty red wool that gave it a festive appearance. She untied the wool and folded back the paper. Out of the corner of her eye Rose saw Poppy half rise from the couch, craning her neck to see what the package contained.

It was a shawl. A triangular cobweb of soft white wool,

warm and light. The shape of a flower had been worked into the back. Rose held it up and heard her sisters gasp. A folded letter fell to her lap. She let the shawl drape across her knees and opened the letter.

She read,

Your Highness,

I thought you might need this, as the days are getting colder. White will look good with your hair, and the scarlet ball gown I've seen you wear in the evenings. I hope it was not too presumptuous of me.

Yours sincerely,
Galen Werner

"What does it say?" Poppy was on her feet now, dancing around in anticipation. "What does it say? Does he love you madly?"

"Poppy," Daisy frowned. "I told you—"

But Poppy was already across the room, holding the shawl up to the light to admire it, putting it down again to reach for the letter. "What does it say?"

Rose snatched the letter out of her sister's reach. "It says that the weather is cold, and he thought I might like a shawl. The end." She refolded the letter and tucked it into her belt.

The words of the letter had been very formal, almost stilted. But she fancied that there was a little hidden warmth there. He had noticed the color of her hair and remembered her red gown.

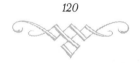

He had taken the time to make her this shawl, and there had been the meetings in the hothouses, the bouquets for them all, and the rose he picked just for her. . . .

"Why are you laughing?" Jonquil came into the sitting room, looking upset.

"Galen, the good-looking under-gardener, is in love with Rose," Poppy said.

"What?" Jonquil frowned around at them, not even seeming to really hear what Poppy had said.

Lily came into the room, looking just as upset as Jonquil. "Have you heard?"

"Heard what?" Rose got to her feet. She took the shawl back from Poppy and, without really thinking about it, swung it around her shoulders. Lily and Jonquil both looked very grave.

"Father has just had a letter from the archbishop," Lily said. Her face was as white as chalk. "He's accusing us of witchcraft. The archbishop is threatening to excommunicate Father and the twelve of us, if it proves to be true." She stretched out her hands to Rose. "The bishop who brought the letter has already taken Anne to his rooms for questioning. I suppose he thinks she's teaching us spells along with geography. Bishop Schelker tried to stop him, but he doesn't have the authority."

The younger set stopped giggling. Poppy stopped trying to snatch the letter out of Rose's belt, and Daisy went pale and swayed where she stood. Rose felt as though all the blood had been drained from her face and hands, and for the second time that day she felt the floor falling out from under her.

"But why?" Rose could barely form the words. "Why?"

King Gregor came into the room just then, one arm around a sobbing Hyacinth. In his free hand he held a long roll of parchment with seals and ribbons hanging from the bottom of it. His skin was gray and waxy. "Why?" he said in a hoarse voice. "Because, according to the kings of Analousia, La Belge, Breton, Spania, and nearly every other nation in Ionia, I not only condone the practice of witchcraft, but used it to kill the princes who refused to marry my daughters."

Hyacinth fainted dead away.

Interdict

Galen was sitting in Zelda's pastry shop, talking to Jutta and her husband, when the news reached the city at large. His cousin, Ulrike, her normally rosy-cheeked face ghastly pale, ran into the shop and skidded to a halt at their table. She clutched Galen's shoulder and panted for a moment while they all stared at her.

"Have you ... have you ... have you heard?" She gasped out the words, her free hand pressed to her side.

"Heard what?" Galen rose to his feet, concerned, and helped the girl into a chair.

Jutta fetched another cup and poured some tea for Ulrike from the pot on their table. "Has there been an accident?"

Galen felt a surge of alarm. "Uncle Reiner? Tante Liesel? What's happened?"

Shaking her head, Ulrike took up the teacup in shaking hands. "A bishop from Roma came with a letter from the archbishop," she said.

"About what?" Galen felt a stirring of dread in his gut.

"They say the royal governess is a witch. She's already been arrested! The archbishop has accused the princesses as well. The letter says they've been using magic to kill all those foreign princes. If they don't confess, they'll be excommunicated. And if they do, it will probably be worse!"

They all sat in shocked silence at this. The ladies seated at the next table had been eavesdropping, and one of them dropped her teacup with a small scream. Soon the room was a hubbub of sound as the news spread to the other tables.

"There's more," Ulrike said, leaning over the table and whispering so that their hysterical neighbors would not hear. "Westfalin has been placed under Interdict."

Jutta shuddered and her husband put his arm around her, his expression horrified. Galen was so busy worrying about Rose that he almost didn't hear.

"Interdict?" he said finally, shaking himself. "You don't mean . . ."

"I do," Ulrike breathed. "No mass. No marriages, no funerals, no christenings. For anyone." Ulrike took a shaky sip of tea and splashed some on her dress in the process. She blotted at the stain with her handkerchief, not really seeming to care.

"The royal governess is a witch?" Jutta frowned. "She comes here from time to time, for tea. She always seemed so kind."

Galen shook his head. "It's a ploy to get the princesses to confess to something they didn't do, to appease the foreign kings. At least you can't execute royalty for witchcraft. Can you?"

"No, but you *can* force a king to abdicate," Jutta said, shaking her head.

Her husband looked at Galen. "Are they guilty, do you think? Have you seen anything suspicious at the palace?"

Galen envisioned little Petunia running shrieking through the hedge maze. It was madness to think of her being a witch. Or delicate Pansy and quiet, gracious Lily. Poppy was a wild one, he thought with a small smile, but he still couldn't believe such a thing of her. And it was certain that her twin, Daisy, and the devout Hyacinth were not witches.

And Rose?

"Impossible," he said, putting down his teacup. "It's impossible for any of those girls—I mean, the princesses—to be witches."

"Well," Jutta's husband said, leaning back in his chair. "It makes sense that something unnatural is afoot, doesn't it?" He was a large, thoughtful man with thick blond hair and a placid expression. "And they won't say what it is, will they? And then these princes come, and try to find out, and they die for their trouble."

Galen clenched his fists. "They are not witches."

Jutta raised her eyebrows at his vehement tone. "You must admit, however, that all these deaths are suspicious." She lowered her voice. "And you've probably never heard the rumors about Queen Maude."

"What rumors?" Ulrike looked curiously at Jutta. "All I've ever heard about her was how much she loved her garden." She wrinkled her nose. "Of course, this all comes from Father,

who probably loves the garden more than the queen and king put together."

"Well"—Jutta looked around to make sure that no one was listening in—"the king and queen didn't have any children for a long, long time. After a while they became very sorrowful over it: they never had any parties, the queen hardly left the Fol— the garden. Then one day, they threw a huge ball and started telling everyone that they *knew* they'd be blessed with a child within the next year. And they were: Princess Rose. And then, after years of being barren, Queen Maude gave birth to twelve daughters, right in a row. Very strange, don't you think?"

This gave Galen pause. Walter had said a few things about the old queen, as well. Could she have used magic to have her twelve daughters? It was very strange, as Jutta said. They sat in silence for a while, sipping tea that had gone cold and crumbling sweet rolls that no one had any appetite for.

"Do they have any other choice?" Galen said finally. "The king must confess to witchcraft or be excommunicated? And if he does confess, isn't the penalty excommunication anyway? And what about the governess? Hanging?" He looked at his cousin.

Ulrike shook her head. Her father had not told her the details, if he even knew them. Then she grimaced. It was clear to all of them that there was little hope for King Gregor and his twelve daughters.

"I'm going to find out more," Galen said. He threw down his napkin and got to his feet. He nodded a farewell to Jutta and her husband, and took his cousin's arm. "You'd better

come home as well." He frowned at the panicky people moving around the shop in restless, gossiping clusters. "In case the city gets out of hand."

Their friends stood as well. "You will tell us, if you find out anything?" Jutta gave him an anxious look.

Galen nodded as he escorted his cousin out of the shop. Signs of unrest were everywhere. Knots of people stood right in the middle of the street, forcing carriages to go around them as they talked. Passing a small church, Galen saw that it was so crowded, the doors could not be shut. Within, a priest could be heard racing through the words of the mass, trying to perform one final service before the Interdict was enforced.

A city guard was nailing an official proclamation to a sign-post a little farther on. People flocked to read it, pushing one another and cursing as feet were stepped on and shawls snagged. Galen's height gave him an advantage. He and Ulrike stood at the back of the crowd, and he read aloud to her the official news of the Interdiction.

It was as they had thought: no more masses, marriages, or christenings. Any bodies buried would have to be buried in unblessed ground, and the last rites could not be delivered. A trusted member of the archbishop's staff was stationed at the palace, to counsel with King Gregor and his daughters.

"And all because of some shoes," Galen murmured as they hurried away.

"What?" Ulrike had to trot to keep up with him.

"This all began because of their shoes being worn out night after night," he said. He had fallen into an easy quick-march

pace. He put an arm around his cousin's waist to help her along. "If someone could just figure out what they do every night." He shook his head in frustration. "I've tried, but I haven't seen a thing."

Ulrike looked at him in shock. "You have? How?"

Galen glanced down at her. "I have permission from the king to roam the gardens at night. I've been sneaking around for days now, but as far as I can tell the princesses aren't leaving the palace." He cleared his throat, uncomfortable. "I've even tried setting traps for them."

"Traps? What kind of traps?"

"Hanging bells in the ivy on the palace walls in case they're using it to climb down, sprinkling flour outside the doors and windows, so that they'll leave tracks. They'd have to fly off the roof like owls to get out of the palace at night without me knowing."

"But think of how many others have tried to find out their secret," Ulrike huffed. "Tried and died. You should be more careful."

"Don't worry—I have an advantage," Galen said, as they arrived on the Orm doorstep.

"What?" Ulrike pressed a hand to her side, panting.

Galen smiled at her and laid a finger to his lips. "It's a secret."

Suitor

Galen's relations clearly thought him to be mad, but he would not be deterred. He washed and dressed in his best clothes. They were actually a shirt and suit of his late cousin Heinrich's that Tante Liesel had altered to fit Galen's slimmer frame, but it was all fairly new and he thought them quite fine. His short hair wasn't long enough to comb, but he tried it anyway, and he polished his boots. All the while Tante Liesel and Ulrike stood in the hallway outside his room and begged him to see reason.

Ulrike sobbed. "You're going to die!"

He opened the door just as Tante Liesel, wringing her hands, was about to say something in the same vein. She stopped when she saw him, however.

"You do look very handsome." She sniffled and brushed at his lapel. "The color suits you. Heinrich looks—looked—well in dark colors too."

The suit was a very dark blue, nearly black. Galen gave her

a smile and a kiss on the cheek, then kissed Ulrike for good measure. In a leather satchel he had the dull purple cloak the old woman had given him. He hadn't showed it to anyone, even though he had been tempted to alleviate his aunt's fears. He knew enough about magic to know that one shouldn't reveal its secrets to others lightly.

At the bottom of the stairs, Uncle Reiner waited.

"What's all this, then?" Reiner's face was haggard and his breath smelled of wine.

"I am going to the palace to speak with King Gregor," Galen said lightly. He didn't really feel as brave or as confident as he acted, but the war had taught him to fake both very well.

"You're getting above your place, lad," Uncle Reiner said. "All this talking in corners with the princesses . . . I should have put a stop to it at once."

"I think I can help them," Galen said quietly.

"You'll not bother them in their time of trouble," Reiner said, putting a restraining hand on Galen's shoulder. "We'll go back to work tomorrow morning as if nothing were amiss, and if I see you so much as look at one of the princesses, I'll have you shoveling manure till doomsday." He squeezed Galen's shoulder, hard. "Understand?"

Galen clenched his jaw. He disliked being manhandled. With a deft twist, he freed himself of Uncle Reiner's grip and moved past the older man to the door. "Good-bye."

As he walked down the street, he heard his uncle shouting about him not being welcome in their house again, but he ignored it. If he wasn't able to solve this puzzle, he would

soon die. And if he was . . . well, perhaps that would help to change Uncle Reiner's mind. Galen did not expect to be extended the same offer that the princes had been given. King Gregor would not want an under-gardener as a son-in-law, and would certainly never designate him his heir.

The gates were locked, and it was only after he had showed his letter from King Gregor to the guards that they let him inside. They sneered at his paltry title at the top of the letter: *Under-gardener Galen Werner*. By way of reply, Galen calmly pointed out to one guard that his powder horn was leaking. Clucking his tongue over this negligence, Galen went up the drive to the front doors of the palace, shrugging aside the guards' shouts to go around the back to the servants' entrance.

Before Galen could knock, he heard someone coming up the steps behind him and turned to see who it was. Walter Vogel stood there, one eyebrow arched as he took in Galen's finery.

"Did you find out something last night?" the old man asked.

"No," Galen said. "But I haven't given up hope yet. I'm here to ask King Gregor if I can't try to solve this from the inside."

"As a potential suitor?"

"As a concerned . . . friend," Galen said.

"Come with me first," Walter said, and stumped off without waiting to see if Galen would follow.

He led Galen to the herb garden near the kitchens. Like all the gardens in the palace grounds, it was beautifully laid out, in a circular pattern with the various herbs planted in wedge-shaped

sections, and neatly raked paths in between. Most of the herbs were long harvested, but Walter moved confidently to the center of the circle and rooted around the base of some tall dill plants that still grew.

"Here you are, young Galen."

Walter presented Galen with a sprig of surprisingly green leaves. A few pale green berries clung to the stem as well.

"What is that?" Galen leaned close and sniffed but couldn't detect an odor.

"Nightshade," Walter replied.

Galen drew back. "Why is it growing here?"

"It's quite a common weed, actually," Walter said. He looked at the little sprig as though he couldn't understand Galen's reaction to it.

"But it's a poison!"

Walter shrugged. "So it is. I'm not proposing that you eat it. Pin a sprig of this under your collar, and it will protect you from enchantment."

"It will?"

"Aye, it will indeed. That's why I let it grow." Walter produced a silver pin from his pocket, looking sly. "A weed, and a poison, but also a powerful help to have around." He offered the sprig to Galen.

Still reluctant to touch it, Galen studied the little plant for a moment. It appeared harmless, but so did any poisonous plant. On the other hand, he trusted Walter. And it would certainly help if he were immune to whatever enchantment haunted the princesses. Not to mention their ill-fated suitors.

He took the nightshade.

Pinning it under his lapel, Galen walked with Walter back around to the front of the palace. There Walter shook Galen's hand solemnly, saying, "Good luck, Galen. *You* are a worthy young man." Then he stumped off on his own business.

Galen didn't want to stand on the doorstep of the palace and ponder Walter's odd remark, so he squared his shoulders and knocked loudly on the tall front door. Herr Fischer, the butler, once again tried to direct Galen around the back, but Galen just smiled and shook his head.

"I'm sorry," Galen told Herr Fischer, "but I'm here on very important business. I really must see the king." He pushed past the short, fussy man and strode into the entrance hall. It was large and grand and scrupulously clean. He fought down the urge to check the soles of his boots and straighten his coat.

"The kitchens are that way," Herr Fischer said, pointing down a narrow passage that led off to the right.

"I didn't come to see the kitchens, thank you," Galen said. "And I can wait as long as need be, but I must see the king."

"Very well." The butler stalked off.

Galen sat in a carved wooden chair at one side of the hall. He put his satchel down at his feet and pulled out a pair of needles and some yarn. He was making himself a stocking cap out of green and brown wool. His current hat was blue, to match his soldier's uniform, and he was heartily sick of it. He began to knit.

A few maids passed him. Their eyes looked swollen, as if from crying, and one of them was clutching a little cross worn

on a chain around her neck. Galen nodded to them pleasantly, and they stared at him.

"Would you mind telling the king that Galen Werner is here to see him?" he called after the maids, knowing full well that Herr Fischer had conveniently "forgotten" his presence. The maids hurried on.

After an hour or so, a large man in purple bishop's robes swept by with a younger, smaller priest trotting at his heels. Galen rose and bowed, but neither man even looked at him. The bishop's eyes were narrow and cold, and a catlike smile played about his lips. Galen guessed him to be the archbishop's emissary and the young priest his assistant.

Shortly afterward, Galen heard quiet voices and the patter of light steps on the gallery above his head. He jumped up and turned around. Princess Violet and Princess Iris walked along the gallery. Their faces, like the maids', were blotchy from crying.

"Hello there, Your Highnesses," Galen called out. When they looked at him, he saluted with his knitting needles.

"Are you here to see Rose?" Iris's voice was tremulous, and she sniffed into a handkerchief.

"No, indeed, ladies. I'm here to speak to your father, King Gregor."

"Why?" Curiosity wiped some of the sadness from Iris's face.

Galen decided that, if he had risked his home and livelihood simply by coming here, he might as well throw everything in. "I've come to ask the king if I may try to solve the

mystery of your worn-out dancing shoes," he called up to them. His voice echoed loudly in the high-ceilinged hall.

"I knew it!" Poppy came flying out of a room along the gallery, her dark curls bouncing and a handkerchief waving like a flag from one hand. "I knew it! You fancy Rose!"

Much to his embarrassment, Galen blushed. "Well, n-no, I just want to help," he stammered. He felt the heat from his blush creeping up to his ears and down his neck to his collar.

"What is going on out here?" Lily came out of the room Poppy had just appeared from, a frown creasing her lovely brow. "Poppy, Iris, Violet! This is hardly the time for . . . May I help you?" She looked down at Galen with a surprised expression.

He realized how he must look, standing on the floor below the princesses, in his secondhand best suit and with a tangle of yarn trailing around his boots.

"I need to speak to your father, if I may, Your Highness," Galen said, blushing even darker beneath his tan. "I—"

Rose appeared at the far end of the gallery. "What is all this to-do about?" she asked in a chiding voice. She saw Galen, stopped, and blushed.

Around her shoulders was the white shawl he had made for her. Galen felt a thrill of pleasure at seeing her wearing it. It looked lovely on her, as he had known it would, but more than that, the way she was holding the edges made him feel as if she were holding his hand.

She put up her chin. "May I help you, um, Galen?" Her voice started out dignified but squeaked on his name.

Catching himself grinning foolishly, Galen cleared his throat and asked again if he might see her father.

Rose's eyes widened. "Why?"

Galen frowned. He didn't think asking to see the king was all that shocking. He had in fact met the king twice in the hothouses.

"I wanted to ask if I could help try to solve the mystery of your worn-out dancing slippers."

Rose flinched and Galen thought he saw a fearful look cross her face. "I'll ask," she said, and went back through the door behind her.

He gathered up his knitting and waited patiently, while the other princesses looked down at him from the gallery. Pansy came out of the door Galen suspected led to the princesses' rooms and stood there looking at him and sucking her thumb for a moment before Lily noticed.

"Pansy! Stop that! You're a big girl!" Lily pulled Pansy's thumb away from her mouth and scrubbed it with a handkerchief. Pansy started to wail.

"Here!" Galen called up to her. "Would you like a ball?"

"No! I hate dancing!" Pansy sobbed.

"I meant a little ball to play with, Your Highness," Galen amended. He was startled by her reaction but covered it by rummaging in his bag. He found some bright red yarn, much cheerier than the brown and green he had been working with, and held it up.

"That's just a wad of yarn," Poppy pointed out.

Galen winked at her. He swiftly wound the yarn around his

left hand a hundred times, cut it, and slipped it off. He tied it in the middle and then used his knife to snip the ends, making a fluffy sort of pom-pom.

"Catch!" He tossed it up to Pansy.

She caught it and looked at it curiously before rubbing the little puff of yarn against her face, her tears stopping. She gave him a watery smile. "Thank you, Herr Under-gardener," she quavered.

Just then Rose came back.

"The king will see you now," she said formally, her face a mask.

Shouldering his bag, Galen went up the curving stairs and joined them on the gallery. He bowed to the princesses assembled there and followed Rose into the room where her father waited. This was a large chamber, mostly filled by a long table and high-backed chairs. There were several men seated around the table, and at its head was the king. He had the deflated look of a plump man who has suddenly lost weight, and there were dark circles under his eyes.

"How is my wife's garden?"

One of the councillors stirred at this. Two others turned and whispered to each other, one of them giving Galen a hard look, as though he thought Galen was wasting their time.

"It flourishes, Your Majesty," Galen said, bowing. "The winter is growing bitter cold, but the snow is not deep. With God's grace, and a gentle spring, we shall have a fine carpet of crocuses."

The king barked a laugh. "God's grace seems to have

abandoned us, son." King Gregor looked Galen over. "You are the young man who has been . . . patrolling the gardens, are you not?"

"Yes, sire." Galen saw the startled look on Rose's face, and on the faces of several of the councillors, and guessed that the king had not told many people about Galen's night-time activities.

"Have you anything to report?"

"Only that the princesses are not leaving the palace, sire." Galen blushed furiously as he said this, seeing the betrayed look in Rose's eyes.

One of the councillors shook his head. "We already know that. The palace guard confirmed that months ago," he said impatiently.

The king didn't respond. His gaze flicked to Rose and the shawl she still clutched about her shoulders. "My daughter Rose says that you may be able to help us."

"Yes, sire." Galen ignored the derisive snorts from the whispering councillor, glancing over at Rose instead. Her brows were drawn together in a worried expression, and when she met his eyes she seemed to be pleading with him. He didn't dare ask her what she was thinking, but plunged ahead. "I would like to try my hand at solving the mystery of the dancing slippers from within the palace. As the late princes have done."

"If the princesses would simply stop being coy," one of the whispering men said, his voice carrying purposefully, "we would have no need of interruption by under-gardeners." His companion snickered.

Angry that this man should dare to speak about Rose in such a tone, Galen addressed him directly. "Do you really think that the princesses would risk their lives, their reputations, simply to play games? Sir?"

The man opened and closed his mouth like a landed trout, his eyes angry. Galen turned his back on him and faced the king again.

"Your Majesty, if you will grant me three nights, I swear that I will solve this riddle or die trying."

"You're certain to die trying," one of the councillors said with a sneer. "Better men than you already have."

Both the king and Galen pretended not to hear, while Galen saw Rose's expression darken out of the corner of his eye. The king studied Galen, and Galen looked back calmly.

"What makes you think that you have an advantage over the young men who have already tried? It's hardly an indication of intelligence or cunning, but they *were* all of royal birth. I do not mean to offend you, young man, but you were given permission to roam the gardens at night because you claimed to have some sort of advantage over my guard. And, well . . ." The king trailed off, spreading his hands.

"I'm sure that the princes were all brave young men," Galen said, although having met some of them, he didn't think that was true at all. "And I would not, of course, expect the same treatment or the reward offered. But I served many years in Your Majesty's army. I fought in battles and was sent on scouting missions to spy on the Analousians. I have been working some months now in the Queen's Garden and am very familiar

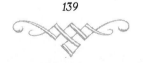

with the exterior of the palace and the grounds. And . . ." He hesitated, and then decided to be "coy," as the councillors would say. "And I have a few other tricks up my sleeve." He laid a finger alongside his nose and winked.

The councillors looked variously annoyed or derisive, but the king just looked thoughtful. "Very good," he said, nodding. "Would you care to start tonight?"

"If it so pleases Your Majesty."

"Indeed it does," the king said. "We shall extend every courtesy to you, of course. It would not be fair, otherwise."

"Your Majesty!" One of the king's advisers rose to his feet, flabbergasted. "You can't mean—"

"You shall join us for dinner," the king said to Galen, talking over his councillor's babble. "You shall have access to my daughters' chambers tonight, chaperoned by their maids, of course."

Galen bowed his head, "Of course."

"And should you succeed . . ." The king pursed his lips. "Well. We'll cross that bridge when we come to it."

Bowing, Galen murmured his thanks. "I shall do my best to help you, Your Majesty. And your noble daughters."

"You'd better," the king said, not unkindly. "Rose, take him to the housekeeper. He shall have a room here for the next few days. You might want to have a rest before this evening. It's going to be a long night." The king looked as if he were going to have a long night as well and rather wished he could take a nap right now.

"Thank you again, sire," Galen said, and bowed his way out of the room. Rose followed.

"Are you mad?" Rose asked as soon as the door closed behind them. "You're going to fail, and then you're going to die!"

But Galen tapped the side of his nose again and winked, even though his heart was racing. It thrilled him that she was concerned for his safety, but he put that out of his head with an effort. He was not trying to take advantage of her or her father while they were under duress from the archbishop.

"You *are* mad!" She stalked down the corridor.

He fell into step beside her. "I think it best if I have a rest, as your father suggested, before dinner," he said in a conversational tone. "If I am to go dancing with you tonight, I want to have all my strength."

Galen's reward for this sally was seeing Rose's cheeks turn bright red.

"I do hope that you will save a waltz for me, Your Highness. I dearly love to waltz. Do you?"

"Not anymore," she said curtly. They had arrived at a small door at the end of a long passageway. She raised one hand to knock and then turned to Galen again. In a low voice she said, "Galen, please reconsider. You are signing your own death warrant by volunteering for this."

He took her raised hand between both of his and squeezed her fist. "I understand that. But I won't let you continue to suffer, Rose."

She closed her eyes, breathing deeply. Then she extracted her hand and knocked. A plump woman in a white apron answered it promptly: the housekeeper had been having a cup of tea in her private sitting room, from the look of things.

"This is the housekeeper, Frau Kramer," Princess Rose said. "Frau Kramer, this young fool is going to try to find out our secret. Please show him to a room." She hurried away, leaving Galen and the housekeeper staring after her.

"I see," Frau Kramer said after a moment. She looked at Galen curiously. "Aren't you the head gardener's nephew?"

"Yes, goodfrau."

"What in the world are you doing in this accursed place?" She shook her head sadly. "You haven't a hope. No one does. They dragged that fancy Bretoner governess off kicking and screaming not four hours ago."

"I know a few tricks," Galen said distractedly. He was still looking down the passageway in the direction Rose had gone. She cared for him! She did!

"Tricks? Of what sort?" She gave him a suspicious look.

"I'm invisible," he said, and then gave a phony laugh to make her think it was a joke.

She didn't find it amusing.

First Night

Rose had been certain that her sisters would behave in a most embarrassing fashion at dinner, but she needn't have worried. While several of them thought it desperately romantic that Galen was risking his life to save them, Anne's arrest and their own impending investigation weighed too heavily on their hearts for them to do any teasing. And there was also the presence of Bishop Angier, the archbishop's emissary, to add to the seriousness of the situation.

Even though this was supposed to be a private family dinner, Angier had included himself, sitting at the foot of the table like a dark cloud. Galen did not try to make conversation, but ate calmly and didn't seem to notice Angier's presence. Rose was relieved to see that Galen had excellent table manners: she hadn't wanted him to embarrass himself in front of Jonquil and Daisy, who were both very critical of such things.

Finally the silence got to the bishop.

"Do you risk your immortal soul, young man?" Angier

had a rasping voice, and a look of malevolent glee contorted his face. He appeared delighted at the thought that Galen might be facing down damnation.

"No, Your Excellency," Galen said. "I don't believe so."

"You have come into a house where sorcery is practiced. Does that not frighten you?" The bishop pursed his thick lips. He was a large man without a single hair on his head. Rose thought he looked like uncooked dough. "It should frighten any God-fearing man."

"I believe that the princesses are innocent," Galen said calmly. "And I am merely here to discover what ill fortune is plaguing them."

Rose marveled at his self-control. She was shredding a roll into tiny bits and doing her best not to shout something rude at Bishop Angier.

Across the table from her, Galen went on. "And with Your Excellency's watchful presence here, I didn't think that my soul could be endangered."

Galen caught Rose's eye and smiled.

"Do you smile, sir?" Angier was indignant. "Smile in the face of the horrors that have gone on here?"

This wiped the amused expressions off everyone's faces. Pansy started to cry, and Petunia dropped her glass and spilled lemonade all over the white tablecloth.

"Your Excellency!" King Gregor flushed red. "There is no need for such talk in front of my daughters! They are too young to understand—"

"They are not too young to perpetrate these atrocities," the

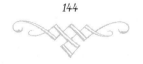

bishop interrupted. Then he corrected himself quickly. "I mean, they are not too young to have been *influenced* by that governess's terrible ways."

Rose stiffened. She knew that poor Anne was being used as a scapegoat in this, but Angier made it obvious that his goal was to defame her family. She wished that he would leave Anne alone and confront her father like a man.

"With all respect, Your Excellency," Galen said in a mild voice, "the only thing you *can* prove the princesses are guilty of is wearing out their shoes too often. None of the princes who have died in recent months met their fate on Westfalian soil. They perished in tragic yet normal accidents. That is, those who didn't die at the hand of another prince."

Poppy rapped on her glass with a knife to applaud Galen's speech. Violet made an appreciative sound at the chiming of the silver on crystal, and began tapping her glass with a fork, her head cocked to one side. She hummed a little, trying to match the note. Iris, Lilac, and Orchid, with relieved expressions, all began tapping their glasses as well, trying to find a melody.

"Girls! Girls!" King Gregor looked shocked.

Rose and Lily exchanged glances. Such behavior was quite appallingly rude, but Rose could see that it was more a reaction to the stresses of the day than a lack of manners. She just shrugged at Lily, who smiled back faintly.

But it was all too much for Hyacinth. She had been stumbling about like a sleepwalker since Angier had arrived. And now the argument with the bishop and the chime of silverware

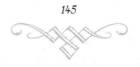

on crystal broke her. She began to sob loudly into her napkin. "Stop it, stop it!"

"Hyacinth!" Rose got to her feet.

"I wish we'd never been born," she wailed. "I wish we'd lost the war, too!" She threw down her napkin and fled the room.

"Very interesting," the bishop said in his shrewd voice, steepling his fingers under his chin. "I wonder what she meant by that." His small, sharp eyes sought out Rose's, and she shuddered.

Recovering quickly, she made a polite curtsy to her father and then to the bishop. "May I be excused? I don't think Hyacinth should be alone."

"I would also like to go to her," Lily said, rising to her feet. The rest of the girls rose as well, and Galen.

"And I should be keeping an eye on them," he said, and bowed to the king and the bishop.

The king dismissed them and they all filed out. Galen took Rose's arm as they went up the stairs to the sisters' rooms. His arm was hard with muscle, and warm through the sleeve of his suit. Rose did her best not to clutch at him like she was drowning.

Inside their sitting room, Galen sat down in an armchair by the fire and took out the whatever it was he was knitting. Hyacinth was huddled in the window seat, weeping piteously. Rose went to her and sat down, pulling Hya into her arms while the other girls clustered around them, making sympathetic noises.

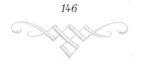

The younger set could not be expected to fuss over Hyacinth forever, though, and they drifted away to talk to Galen. Rose noticed that he was endlessly patient with them, not minding when Petunia unrolled one of his skeins of yarn to play cat's cradle with the end. He sat Pansy on the arm of his chair and showed her how to knit.

Rose went over and sat in the chair across from Galen. He looked up at her, smiled, and went back to coaching Pansy, who finally set the puff ball he'd made for her aside to better use the needles. Mewing like a cat, Petunia came over and started to wind yarn around Rose's skirts.

"So," Rose said, and then couldn't think of anything to say. "What was the war like?" she asked finally, feeling like a fool.

A shadow passed over Galen's face, making Rose regret her question. "It was"—he glanced at Pansy's bent head—"it was not pleasant," he said shortly.

"I'm sorry, I didn't mean to open any old wounds," she said, contrite.

"Wounds? Were you ever injured?" Orchid came over, her eyes wide with curiosity.

"A few times," Galen replied. "Nothing serious."

"Oh." She sounded almost disappointed. "Walter Vogel lost a leg. But he says it wasn't in the Analousian war."

"I know."

Orchid pursed her lips. "Do you think it hurt?"

"I'm sure it did," Galen said grimly.

"Were you with your cousin Heinrich?" Orchid persisted. "Did you see him die?"

Galen looked up, clearly startled. "Did you know Heinrich, Your Highness? I never met him."

"Of course," Orchid said. "We all knew Heinrich. *Especially* Lily."

Rose interrupted before Orchid could say anything else. "Orchid, your hair is coming out of its ribbons. Why don't you find Maria and have her fix it?" She smiled stiffly at Galen. "Maria is our chief maid."

Grumbling, Orchid went into one of the bedrooms. She returned a moment later. "She's asleep on Iris's bed," she reported. "And she's snoring."

"Oh, dear." Rose glanced at the clock. "No wonder, it's nearly eleven."

"Shouldn't your maids wait up for you?" Galen raised one eyebrow.

"Well, yes, but she can't because . . ." Rose's voice died in her throat, courtesy of the enchantment. She closed her mouth with a snap and looked at Galen. He gazed mildly back at her without the slightest sign of sleepiness. Her eyes widened and her mind raced.

Why hadn't he fallen asleep as well? What were they to do if he was wide awake at midnight? Hope rose in her bosom. If Galen could resist the sleeping spell that had affected all the other suitors, then he might be able to uncover their secret and . . . what? Die horribly? She grimaced, her hope fading.

"Is something the matter?" Galen gave her a bland look.

"Oh, look at the time!" Jonquil jumped to her feet, almost knocking Hyacinth off the window seat. "I've got to change

my shoes and—*Why is he awake?*" She pointed in horror at Galen. Then she got ahold of herself, dropped her arm, and looked helplessly at Rose.

"If you'll excuse us, I believe I need to talk to my sisters." Rose smiled ingenuously at Galen as she untangled the yarn from her feet. She grabbed Petunia with one hand and Pansy with the other and all but ran into her bedroom. The rest of her sisters followed.

"He's awake! It's eleven o'clock!"

"Jonquil, keep your voice down," Rose hissed. "Yes, he's awake. I don't know how or why, but he is." She looked around. "Poppy, make sure he doesn't eavesdrop."

Grinning, Poppy went over to the door and opened it the barest crack. "He's still sitting in the chair," she whispered. "He put his yarn down, though, and he's leaning back . . . he just yawned!"

Rose was a little suspicious of this, but she didn't tell her sisters.

"There, you see?" Lily looked relieved. "It was just that Pansy and Petunia were climbing around him. That kept him awake. Now he'll sleep and we can rest easy."

"But . . ." Rose hesitated. "What if he did find out the truth?" Even speaking the words made her heart pound. "Would that be so bad?"

They all stared at her.

"Rose," Lily said cautiously. She took Rose's arm and led her away from the others. "Rose, what are you saying? There's nothing he can do to help us—no mortal can. He's in grave

enough danger as it is. If he learned the truth . . ." Lily shook her head sadly. "I hate to think what *he* would do if Galen tried to help us."

"But we *need* help," Rose said, her voice low and intense. "We can't go on like this for six more years! Every night while we were ill we had to get dressed and dance until dawn; we're lucky to have survived! Pansy is seven years old; she's been dancing every night since she could walk. Another year and her sanity will break, I swear it. And you, can *you* keep on this way?"

"We don't have a choice," Lily said, shaking her head. Pansy had begun whimpering at Rose's vehement words, and Lily picked her up and held her, though she was really too big for such treatment. "We must persevere. There's no point in arguing about it, and neither Galen nor anyone else can help us. It's folly to even let him try." Lily paused, then asked delicately, "You do realize that this is a death sentence for him, don't you?"

"No." Rose shook her head. "Not Galen. He's not like those useless princes. He knows how to fight, how to work. You of all people should appreciate that, Lily. Even if he doesn't find a way to help us, he'll survive."

"I hope you're right," Lily said dubiously, but her cheeks had colored a little and a spark of hope lit her eyes. "Galen does remind me of . . . of Heinrich."

Rose squeezed her arm.

"He's asleep," Poppy reported. "His head kept bobbing up and down for a while, but now he's out cold and snoring."

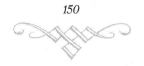

"Good, let's get ready," Jonquil said, and she flounced over to her dressing table to arrange her hair.

⬥⬥⬥

An hour later, when the sisters had all tied on their dancing shoes and arrayed themselves in their usual finery, Galen was sound asleep. Rose went over to him and tapped his shoulder, but he just snored on and she turned away.

Galen's wing chair was turned toward the fire, so that the rug in the center of the room was mostly behind him. Still, Rose watched him nervously as Lily opened the secret entrance. His head had lolled against one of the wings in such a way that if he were to suddenly wake, he would be able to see them out of the corner of his eye. Lily went down the spiraling staircase first, and the rest of the sisters followed after. Still tense, Rose brought up the rear as they filed down into the darkness for the Midnight Ball.

Twigs

As soon as Rose's head passed down into the floor and out of sight, Galen leaped to his feet, yanked the purple cape out of his satchel, and threw it around his shoulders. Hugging the satchel close to his chest, he hurried after her. The portal in the floor brushed his close-cropped hair as it closed, and he bit back a curse.

He had feigned sleep, even though he was so keyed up that he couldn't imagine closing his eyes. He'd worried that the snoring was a bit much but knew that he couldn't stop once he'd started, and it seemed to convince the princesses.

Except for Rose. Rose was far too clever.

When she came up to touch his shoulder, he was terrified that she would see him peeking at them from under his lashes. In his relief when she turned away, he had almost forgotten to continue snoring. And then, incredibly, the rug had turned into a staircase leading down into the floor.

Rose stopped suddenly, and Galen nearly ran into her.

"What was that?" Her voice was breathless with fright. She spun around and Galen tensed, but she peered right through him.

"What's the matter?" Lily called from the front of the line.

"I thought I heard footsteps. Heavy footsteps," Rose said. "I feel like someone is following me."

Lily held her lamp higher. "There's no one there, Rose. How could there be?" She continued on down the steps, and the other princesses followed her.

"Just a draft, I suppose." Rose sighed.

Galen did his best to creep silently down the stairs after that, breathing into the collar of his cape so that he wouldn't blow on Rose's neck. At last they came to the foot of the golden staircase, and Galen gaped at what lay before them.

All around was darkness, darkness that their lamp only dimly illuminated. But directly in front of them was a tall gate made of silver and set with pearls the size of pigeon's eggs. There was no fence, only a gate, and beyond it a forest of strange pale trees.

Lily swung open the gate and the princesses passed through, with Galen at Rose's heels. He dodged to the side as she turned and shut the gate behind them, closing the pearl-inlaid latch, and then they went forward into the forest.

To find a forest in this strange underground world was odd enough, but this was no ordinary forest. The trees were of shining silver, their branches spreading high into the blackness above them and glowing with their own light. The leaves rattled and chimed together, moved by a breeze that somehow

did not touch the humans: Galen's cape was not stirred by any wind and the princesses' hair was not ruffled.

Galen stared around in amazement at the forest, but the princesses passed through without comment. He realized that they must see this every night, and it no longer amazed them, if it ever had. The forest, then, was not their reason for coming.

The silver trees thinned and then stopped, and they were on the shore of a great lake. Beneath their feet coarse black sand glittered, and the water that lapped the shores was black and violet and deepest blue. Twelve golden boats with a single lantern hanging from each bow were drawn up on the sand, tethered to twelve tall statues.

Then one of the statues moved, and again Galen found himself hard-pressed not to curse aloud. They weren't stone, but living beings: tall young men, stern of face and black of hair, dressed in ebony-hued evening clothes. Galen hesitated to call them human, however. There was something amiss in their bearing, in their pallor and the coldness of their expressions. With a start Galen recognized one of the figures as the creature the girls had referred to as Rionin, who had tried to climb into the princesses' rooms weeks ago.

Surely nothing human could live in this sunless world, Galen thought. Whatever Rionin and his companions were, they were not mortal.

One by one the princesses took the proffered hands and were helped into a golden boat. Galen waited until Rose's dark-haired suitor had seated her in the bow and was about to

push off into the strangely colored lake. Then Galen stepped into the boat and sat on the empty stern seat.

Each of the silent escorts sat in the middle seat and took up the golden oars. In perfect synchronicity, the twelve boats set out across the lake, the suitors rowing silently as one.

Their precision was somewhat ruined by Rose's rower, however. Halfway across the lake he slowed, and Galen heard him pant a little.

"Is something wrong?" Rose had been gazing forward, but now she looked back at her escort.

"The boat seems a little heavier this time," the rower said. His voice was deep and smooth.

Rose blushed. "Sorry," she muttered. Galen stifled a laugh.

Ahead of them Galen now saw lights glimmering in the blackness. They did little to illuminate the lake, but the purplish flickers ahead showed that they were rapidly approaching... something.

The golden boats scraped on more gritty black sand, and at last Galen could see the source of the strange light. It was a great palace of slick black rock. The candlelight that flickered in the windows gleamed purple because the panes too were black.

One by one the princesses were helped out of the boats, and one by one they passed through the great arched doors and into the black palace. Hard on Rose's heels, Galen followed. His palms were wet with sweat, but he focused on her slim back and reminded himself that he was invisible to the cold eyes of her escort.

Within the palace, the colors were much the same as the

water of the underground lake. Purple and blue and gray and black tapestries covered the walls. The floor and ceiling were gleaming black, and the furniture was made of silver, cushioned with silk in the same solemn colors as the tapestries.

They passed through a long hall and into a ballroom where amethyst chandeliers hung over a floor inlaid with silver and lapis lazuli. Musicians played in a gallery so high above their heads that Galen could barely make out their forms, and servants in black livery passed among the guests with trays bearing silver goblets of wine. When the princesses arrived, the guests all stopped dancing and talking and applauded them. The grim suitors bowed, the princesses curtsied, and the musicians struck up a lively tune. Rose and her sisters were whirled away, leaving Galen alone and unseen to watch.

Glad that no one could see him gaping like a half-wit, Galen wandered through the ballroom. It was a wonder that the sisters had seemed so reluctant to come here, their faces strained and Pansy frankly in tears. What young girl wouldn't love to dance away her nights in this splendid castle, in the arms of a handsome suitor?

But as he roamed the edge of the dance floor, Galen started to think that it was not as beautiful here as he had first thought. The other people at the ball all smiled and sipped their wine and danced, but their smiles were not . . . quite . . . right. Their lips stretched too wide, and they seemed to have too many teeth. Their eyes glittered like the jewels they wore, and their skin was too white and smooth.

And then still there were the princesses. They danced. They ate delicate pastries and strange fruits.

But they did not smile.

Hyacinth wept, the tears running silently down her cheeks as she whirled around the floor in the arms of her tall partner. Pansy sobbed noisily, and occasionally stopped dancing to stomp on her partner's feet. He wore a look of long-suffering, and after a few dances he simply picked her up and carried her around the floor, swaying in time to the music.

"Do they *have* to dance?" Galen said aloud without thinking. The white-faced woman standing near him narrowed her eyes and stared right at the spot where Galen stood. Holding his breath, he backed away.

Galen remembered how Pansy had burst into tears earlier when he had offered her a "ball." He thought about Rose's illness, and how it had continued for months while her slippers were worn out night after night. Surely she would not have come here to dance in the extremity of her illness unless she had no other choice. The one night they hadn't danced, Rionin and his brethren had invaded the garden.

But why? Who was forcing them to come here?

An hour later, this question was answered. The music stopped, and the dancers all turned to look expectantly at a tall door at the far end of the room. The musicians played a long fanfare, and the door opened to reveal a tall man wearing a long black robe and a crown tarnished blue-black.

"All hail the King Under Stone," one of the footmen

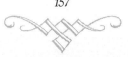

shouted. He banged a silver staff on the floor three times. "All hail the king!"

"All hail the king!" the guests chanted in reply.

As the man stepped into the room, Galen swallowed thickly. If the smiles and eyes of the courtiers had made Galen nervous, the appearance of their king made him break out in a cold sweat.

Skin as white as paper, taller and thinner than anyone Galen had ever seen, the king of the underground palace surveyed his court with eyes like chips of obsidian. His thin lips peeled back from sharp white teeth in a hideous parody of a smile.

"So nice to see that my sons' brides-to-be have at last recovered their strength," the king said in a wintry voice. "It is always so refreshing to see our royal flowers in bloom." His cold eyes rested on Rose. "Our dear Rose, especially."

Without thinking, Galen's hand went to his hip where once he had worn a pistol. He bit his tongue, though, and forced himself to relax so that he would not give away his presence.

The King Under Stone. Rose and her sisters were prisoners of the King Under Stone. Galen's knees almost buckled. There wasn't a mother in Ionia who hadn't frightened her children into obedience by using that name, or who hadn't prayed over the same child so they might never encounter that evil being.

He was the stuff of nightmares, the stuff of campfire tales. A magician so steeped in evil that he had ceased to be human, transforming himself and his most devout followers into something *other*: immortal and monstrous. According to legend, centuries ago every country on the continent of Ionia had risen up against him and cast him into an underground prison. He

was too powerful to be destroyed completely, and trapping him in a sunless realm with only his followers to rule over had been the only solution. An army of white witches had been gathered to do the deed, and the effort had cost many of them their lives. It was a legend everyone knew.

And now it appeared that the legend was true.

The King Under Stone glided across the floor to the dais and sat on his tall throne. "Please, continue dancing. You know how much I enjoy the dancing."

The court tittered at this, and the king clapped his long, thin hands. The musicians began a jig, and Under Stone sat, immobile, his long silver hair hanging down either side of his skeletal face, and watched the princesses.

Pansy's partner had at last given in and allowed her to sit in a chair to one side of the room, asking one of the hard-faced court women to dance instead. Galen sidled across the room and sat in the empty chair beside the young princess.

"Paaaaansy," he whispered in a hollow voice. "Don't moooove. I am a gooooood spirit!"

Pansy sat up straight and whimpered, her eyes flickering around as she searched for the source of the voice. "Who's there?"

"I'm a good spirit," Galen repeated. "I want to help yooooou."

She bit her lip, tears leaking from the corners of her reddened eyes. Galen's heart went out to her. This poor child was clearly beyond the edge of her endurance, but he didn't dare to put his arm around her. For one thing, good spirits did not

wear heavy wool suits, and for another, he didn't want anyone to see Pansy's shoulders turn invisible.

"Why do you come here?" Galen asked.

Pansy wrinkled her nose. "We have to," she said in a matter-of-fact voice. She blinked, looking around again for the good spirit.

"But why?"

"Because of Mother, I guess."

"What did your mother dooooo?" Galen pressed.

"Pansy, get up!" Poppy had appeared in front of them. She had an anxious look on her face. She grabbed her little sister's hands and pulled Pansy off the chair. Poppy glanced nervously over her shoulder to where her partner stood in conversation with Pansy's. "You have to dance again!"

"I'm tired," Pansy whined.

"We're all tired," Poppy snapped. "But we still have to dance."

"But Telinros said—"

"Telinros doesn't matter," Poppy said. "Look at the king!" She jerked her head at the king, who was frowning in their direction. "You've sat out one dance; that's the most any of us get. Come along." And she led the drooping Pansy back to her partner.

From his chair, Galen watched Poppy and Pansy enter the dance once more. Rose whirled by with her suitor, and Galen briefly considered sticking out one of his boots and tripping the dark prince. He decided against it, though, since Rose might fall and hurt herself.

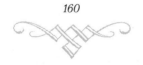

Galen sat back and observed. As the glittering court went around and around the dance floor, his eyes were drawn to the king. The King Under Stone sat even straighter on his throne. His eyes were shining and his white hair and skin had become silvery. As his courtiers and the princesses faded with exhaustion, the king appeared to become stronger, his skin almost glowing.

"He's feeding off their energy," Galen murmured, sickened. How had Queen Maude become embroiled in this? Had she been one of the courtiers? And why had her daughters become enslaved to the King Under Stone?

He found that he couldn't watch the king, or even the dancers, too closely. The whole spectacle sickened him. He let his eyelids slip halfway down and watched the feet of the dancers as they whirled by.

The striking of a great gong woke Galen some time later, and he realized that he had dozed off. Looking around frantically, he spotted Rose, and then quickly counted to make sure that the other princesses were there as well. The king had risen from his throne, rejuvenated, and the courtiers were assembling before him. The princesses with their partners came to stand in a space cleared for them in front of the dais.

"Another night has passed away," the pale king intoned. "Far above us in the mortal world dawn arrives in the kingdom of Westfalin. Two favors did I grant Queen Maude in return for four and twenty years dancing in my court. She gave me fourteen years before her death, five years and fifty-three days of payment remain. And then, my sons, you shall

wed your princesses and keep them here to delight us forever."

The court clapped their pale hands and laughed their shivery laughs. The king's dark sons smiled down at the princesses with a proprietary air, but the princesses merely stood, exhausted and silent. Galen edged around the crowd and stood behind Rose. Her head turned slightly, as though she heard him approach, but she said nothing.

The dark suitors led the princesses away then, through the long hallway and out the tall doors, to crunch down the black sand to the golden boats. Once more Galen hopped into the boat after Rose, and once more her suitor lagged behind the others, a disgruntled expression on his face.

At the far shore of the lake, the suitors helped the princesses out of the rowboats but would not take one step farther toward the forest. The princesses continued on alone, without looking back, into the silver trees.

Trailing behind Rose, Galen thought about what he would tell King Gregor. How to explain where the princesses went every night? How to tell the king that his late, lamented wife had made some sort of bargain with the strange, cold king of this underground realm? The princesses could not speak to support his story, and it was very likely that the king would not believe him.

As they passed beneath the gleaming, otherworldly trees, Galen reached up and snapped off a pair of twigs. The sharp cracking noise made Rose stop dead in her tracks, and she turned around, wildly searching for whatever had made the sound.

"What was that?"

"Rose?" Up ahead, lamp once more in hand, Lily turned and looked down the line of girls. "Are you all right?"

Galen stood very still, holding the twigs beneath his cape. They were cold, and very slick and hard. If he didn't know better, he would say that they really *were* silver, and not the product of a tree at all.

"Didn't you hear it?" Rose squinted at the trees. "There was a loud cracking sound!"

"I didn't hear anything," Lily said, her usually gentle voice impatient. "Let's go! The maids and your gardener will wake soon."

"I heard it too," Orchid said. She was standing just in front of Rose. "Maybe one of the branches broke."

The sisters all looked at the black ground around the trees, but no glint of silver from a broken branch or even a fallen leaf could be seen. Petunia got down on her hands and knees and crawled around the base of the nearest tree.

"Petunia, stop that!" Iris hauled the youngest sister to her feet. "You're getting filthy!"

Black mud that sparkled faintly in the light from Lily's lamp covered Petunia's skirt and the toes of her ruined dancing slippers.

Daisy was hopping from foot to foot. "We have to go," she said. "We've never been this late: the staircase is already there. What if it goes away again before we set home?"

Slipping the twigs into the pouch hanging from his belt, Galen strode after the princesses as they trotted through the

woods and passed under the pearl-studded arch. Rose shut the gates behind them, nearly catching the tail of Galen's cape as he slid through. With a jolt Galen realized that they would expect to see him sleeping in the chair before the fire when they came up through the floor. He sprinted past the princesses, making Lily's lamp flicker as he passed, and took the golden stairs two at a time, trying his best not to make too much noise even as he raced ahead of them.

"What was that?" he heard one of them cry out as he passed.

Galen yanked off the cape and shoved it into his satchel as he dropped into the chair. He fought to turn his panting breath into snores even as, from beneath his lashes, he saw Lily's head rise up out of the black square in the floor. She came at once to his side and peered down at him, checking to see if he was still asleep. As the lamplight fell on his face, he snorted and shifted in his chair but didn't open his eyes.

"Is he still asleep?" Rose whispered.

"Yes," Lily whispered back.

Galen listened as they rustled about, helping each other undress and go into their separate bedrooms to catch a few precious hours of sleep. When they had left the sitting room, he took out his cape and refolded it so that it fit into the satchel better. Then he stretched and found a more comfortable position in the chair, to sleep a little bit himself. He had a lot to think about, but he was far too tired to reason it out now.

"I don't know how they can do it night after night," he mumbled as he drifted off. "Poor Rose...."

Needles

A maid woke Galen, her eyes alight with a question. Galen paused, and then shook his head, assuming a sorrowful expression. She sighed and patted his arm. He went down the hall to the room set aside for him to freshen up before breakfast.

Breakfast was another solemn affair, with Bishop Angier at one end of the table, a stern expression on his face, and King Gregor at the other, looking mournful. Dr. Kelling also joined then, his face anxious. All three men watched Galen carefully, looking for a sign of some small success, but Galen ate and chatted with the princesses as casually as he could. While he had been in his little room, dressing, he had come to a conclusion: he would not say a word until the third night was completed.

The silver twigs gave him some proof of where he had been, but he didn't know how to proceed from there. Galen suspected that merely telling the king where his daughters had been would do nothing to help them. The spell that was over them was powerful indeed, controlling them not only when they entered the underworld, but outside it as well. Otherwise they would have told their father by now. Galen's hope was that, after three nights of following them, he would have learned enough to work out a plan that would free the princesses.

"Galen, please come to my study," King Gregor said wearily when breakfast was over.

"I shall accompany you," Angier said. He heaved his bulk upright and preceded the king and Galen across the hall and into the king's private study. Dr. Kelling made as if to follow, but Angier dismissed him with a gesture. King Gregor began to protest, but the doctor shook his head.

The king sat in the chair behind the desk and the bishop took the comfortable chair before it. Galen stood calmly between them. His soldier's training proved valuable here as it had so many times before: he was nervous, he was uncertain what to do next, but he would never let it show. With an impassive face and ramrod-straight spine, Galen reported to the king and the bishop that, after entering the princesses' chambers, he had sat and talked with them for a while. Then, sometime before midnight, he had fallen asleep and not woken until a little after dawn. The princesses had all been in their beds, very peacefully asleep, but their slippers were worn through once more.

The king threw up his hands in despair. Had Galen been alone with the king, he would have been tempted to give the man some hint of hope, but he refused to do so in front of Angier. The bishop spoke Westfalian with a faint accent, and it had only been at breakfast that Galen had realized it was Analousian. Although as a man of the church he was supposedly above such politics, it still made Galen nervous. Galen bowed himself out of the study and went to find Walter.

The peg-legged gardener was cleaning leaves out of a fountain shaped like a dejected-looking mermaid. The water had been drained, lest it freeze and crack the pipes, and now the empty marble bowl was a catchall for stray leaves and other debris.

Walter greeted Galen with a nod. "How fare our princesses?" the old man inquired.

"Not well," Galen said bluntly. He pushed back the sleeves of his good jacket and bent down to help gather the leaves into a basket.

Walter stopped and sat on the edge of the fountain. "The nightshade worked," he stated.

"It seems so," Galen said, "Tell me: what do you know of a black palace far underground, guarded by a gate of silver set with pearls, surrounded by a forest of silver trees, and built on an island in the middle of a black lake?"

Walter's weathered face went white. "Foolish woman," he breathed. "So she made a bargain with *him.*"

"Rose and the others—" Then Galen stopped. "Then you know of it?" He stared at Walter, angry. "Why didn't you help them?"

Walter shook his head. "I didn't know that Maude had gone so far. I knew that she had summoned help from some unseen source. But I didn't know it was *him.*" Kicking his peg leg against the base of the fountain, Walter looked off into the distance. "Not *him.*"

Galen ran his hand over his short hair. "So Queen Maude really . . . ?"

"Wanted children so badly that she made a pact with the King Under Stone?" Walter sucked his teeth. "So it seems. And I've no doubt that she meddled again, to make certain we won the war."

Galen rejected this, shaking his head. "But we fought hard for that war. It took twelve years—"

"No one ever said that *he* plays fair," Walter interrupted. "Creatures without honor—without souls—never do. Why should they? That's something that Maude never could understand. Ask such a being for strong children, he promises you a dozen, and you strike the bargain. And bear a dozen girls. Ask him to end the war, and he agrees readily . . . then takes twelve years to get around to it."

Galen frowned. "But when the queen died, wouldn't her bargain have become void?"

"Not as far as *he* is concerned, it seems. If she's not there to pay, then her daughters will." Walter hesitated. "So they are dancing for him?"

Galen nodded. "They danced from midnight to dawn with twelve tall young men. I believe they are his sons."

The older man gave a low whistle. "So that's his game, is it?" he said thoughtfully, staring into the distance. "Perhaps he meant to have them all along."

"Walter," Galen said, feeling almost hesitant about asking. "How do you know all this?"

The old man looked at him. The news that the King Under Stone had a hold on the princesses had shaken him, and he looked immeasurably old suddenly. "I have not always been a gardener, Galen Werner," he said drily.

"Then tell me how to stop this."

"Alone? And with twelve sons to aid him?" Walter shook his head. "It will take time."

"We don't have time," Galen argued. "Rose . . . Little Pansy . . . They don't have time, Walter."

"I did not think Maude had gone so deep," Walter was muttering, to himself more than Galen. "And you say its every night now. . . . He must need them more, or is preparing for something. There aren't enough of us left to put a tighter seal on his prison. . . ."

"Walter!" Galen shook the old man's shoulder gently. He lifted his lapel and showed Walter the wilted sprig of night-shade. "I'm going to need more nightshade, at the least. There is a sleeping spell laid over anyone who comes into the princesses' rooms at night," Galen explained. "But it did not affect me as it had the princes."

"Ah!" Walter nodded sagely, his eyes coming into focus again. "So that's how the princesses slip away from their minders." He frowned. "But weren't the girls suspicious? And how is it that you could follow them?"

"They were suspicious at first," Galen admitted. "But then I feigned sleep, and that satisfied them. As to how I was able to follow them . . . that's a secret."

Walter nodded again. "It's good to have secrets."

Together he and Galen gathered up the basket of leaves and set off for the gardener's sheds. Galen dumped the leaves in the mulch pile and put the basket away. Then Walter beckoned, and Galen followed him to the herb garden.

Walter picked another sprig of nightshade, to replace the wilted one. Then he broke off a sharply scented sprig of dried basil and gave it to Galen as well.

"Nightshade will clear the enchantments from your eyes, and enable you to see the truth. And basil wards off evil," he explained.

"Thank you." Galen tossed his wilted nightshade aside and carefully pinned the new sprig in place. Then he put the more brittle basil in the breast pocket of his coat.

As he fumbled with his clothes, the pouch at Galen's belt swung forward and one of the silver twigs sticking out caught on his shirt. Cursing, Galen freed the twig and tried to get it to fit better in the little drawstring bag.

"What are those?" Walter squinted at them.

"A little something that I took from the forest of silver," Galen replied. Checking to make certain that they were alone, he pulled the twigs out of the bag and showed them to Walter.

Turning them over in his gnarled hands, Walter pursed his lips. "Interesting," he said. "These weren't part of his realm, at least not in the beginning." He gave them back to Galen. "Interesting."

"How do you know what his realm is like?"

Walter merely echoed the words he'd said to Galen earlier:

"It's good to have secrets." Then he paused. "But I will say this: silver has power, and so do names."

"Names and silver..." Galen studied the twigs himself. They were long and straight, and the place where they had broken from the larger branch showed little silvery fibers that were some strange hybrid of metal and wood never before seen in the mortal world. "I should have broken off bigger pieces, to make arrows. Or a spear. Something more useful than just taking a souvenir to show King Gregor." He snorted. "They'd make beautiful knitting needles, though."

"Keep them handy," Walter said. "You never know what you'll have need of, when you're in the palace."

Something about Walter's words rang in Galen's ears. The phrasing reminded him of something, and he paused a moment to remember what, but Uncle Reiner came crunching down the gravel path just then. His face darkened when he saw Galen standing with Walter.

"Shouldn't you be inside?" he demanded. "They haven't thrown you out, have they?"

"No, indeed, Uncle," Galen said respectfully. "I have just come to speak with Walter about something." He slid the twigs into his pouch and pulled his coat closed over them.

"Nothing here is of concern to you anymore," Uncle Reiner said. "Be off with you."

Galen nodded politely to his uncle and Walter, and then he took himself off.

Inside the palace, he discovered that the younger princesses were having their lessons with the priest who had accompanied

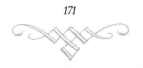

Angier. The older girls were with their father, being questioned by the bishop himself. At loose ends, Galen sat down in his room to finish knitting his hat, but he couldn't get the silver twigs out of his head. Studying them from every angle, he concluded that while they might be whittled down to make darts or something of the sort, they were otherwise useless. But whittling them down would change their shape in such a way that they might not be recognizable as twigs, and therefore unusable as evidence.

"They'll make fine knitting needles, just as they are," Galen said aloud.

He thought for a long time. He could not fight the twelve suitors alone. Besides being outnumbered, who knew what help their father might send. He couldn't break the spell that bound the princesses. . . . He didn't know what exactly it was, and he had no skill with magic besides. If he could just stop them from going to the ball . . . But then the King Under Stone would likely send someone to fetch them again. And this time, Galen doubted that Rionin and the other princes would let a rowan switch deter them.

There had to be a way to fight them, or to stop them from coming aboveground ever again.

As Galen's mind turned the problem over and over, he remembered what Walter's words had reminded him of: the crone.

When you are in the palace, you will have great need.

He broke the silver twigs in half so that there were four pieces, each about the length of his hand. He used his knife to

pare away any jagged edges or splinters that might catch on the wool. Then he pulled out the black wool that the crone had given him.

Black like iron . . .

Galen began to knit.

Second Night

Rose's day did not go well. She had a headache, and her cough had returned. As if to aggravate both problems, she was forced to spend the day in the council chamber, being alternately questioned and lectured by Bishop Angier. His voice made her head pound, and her throat was sore from trying to hold back the coughs.

Having their country placed under Interdiction was a serious thing, and there had already been repercussions. Reports had been arriving all day, and they were not comforting. There had been riots in other cities when the archbishop's edict was read. In Bruch, many people were packing to leave, hoping to immigrate to any neighboring land that would take them. Several grocers and livery stables had been robbed for supplies by those fleeing, and rocks had been thrown at the palace gates and even at the Orms' distinctive pink house.

Rose had hoped that her younger sisters would escape the

bishop's ranting since they had their lessons. And during that time they did, to some extent. But it seemed that the bishop had given his assistant quite stern advice about what the princesses ought to learn.

"I thought I would die," Poppy said dramatically, flinging herself across Rose's bed. "As if it wasn't bad enough that we had to have some pinch-faced priest teaching us instead of Anne, you should hear what he's teaching! Mathematics: gone. Science: gone. History: religious history and lives of the saints only. Literature: more lives of the saints." She put a pillow over her face and howled through the muffling feathers.

"There is nothing wrong with a religious education," Hyacinth reprimanded her, coming into the room.

"There is when you are taught nothing but," Violet argued. She was shredding the edges of her handkerchief. "There's to be no more music," she said in a soft voice. "None at all. Father Michel says . . . he says that we are not serious minded enough to learn even religious music." She bit her lip, her eyes filling with tears. "He's locked my pianoforte and taken the key."

"Oh, darling!" Rose put her arms around Violet, and the younger girl sobbed onto her shoulder.

"He's a nightmare," Poppy said, taking the pillow off her face. "Horrible, odious man! And he's Analousian, too, just like the bishop." A calculating look crossed her face. "You don't think Angier is just trying to humiliate us because they lost the war, do you?"

Hyacinth drew herself up, shocked. "The archbishop would

not have sent someone capable of such pettiness, Poppy," she declared. "We have been charged with witchcraft; this has nothing to do with politics!"

"I don't care if it's politics or not," Violet wailed. "I can't be cut off from my music!"

Rose gave her an extra squeeze.

"Don't worry," Petunia said cheerfully. "Galen will fix everything."

"Oh, he will, will he?" Rose gave a brittle laugh at Petunia's firm statement.

At the same time, though, she hoped in her heart that Petunia was right. She and Lily had searched for years for a way to escape the King Under Stone, reading their mother's diaries over and over for clues, looking up any reference to Under Stone and his banishment that they could find. But the only books they could find about him were legends, and several of their mother's diaries were missing. Rose suspected that the missing diaries were the ones that would have been the most useful, and she wondered if her mother had destroyed them or if Under Stone had found some way to confiscate them.

The sisters had tested all the physical boundaries of his realm, even asking the dark princes to carry them through the forest when they were tired, to see how close to the gate they could get. They had asked as many questions of the courtiers and the dark princes as they dared, and they had found not a single weak spot. They had tried to tell their father, their governess, anyone who would listen, about the curse, but always their lips snapped shut, or they even found themselves spouting nonsense when they tried to talk about it.

For a time they had given up, hoping that they would be able to simply serve out their term below. But soon after the war ended, the King Under Stone had begun to refer to them as his sons' brides, filling the girls with new horror. He was going to find a way to keep them there forever. Now Rose and her sisters needed help more than they ever had before, and Galen was so strong and sure that it seemed almost possible for him to "fix everything." Rose hitched her white shawl a little higher on her shoulders and led Violet over to her dressing table. "Come now, dry your eyes. Let's get ready for dinner."

But Bishop Angier had other plans. When the twelve sisters presented themselves in the dining room, modestly clad in high-waisted, high-necked frocks of somber hues, they found their father and Galen already seated at a table that bore a white cloth, a Bible, and nothing else.

"Sit down," Bishop Angier said.

The princesses sat.

For some two hours the bishop held forth with great animation on the subject of witchcraft and its evils. He also veered into the evil natures of all women, witches or not, and how their fathers and husbands should keep them under firm control. It was vastly different from one of Bishop Schelker's sermons. The most disconcerting part was that Angier would fix his eyes firmly on the face of each sister in turn, and focus on her for minutes at a time. As he locked gazes with Rose for

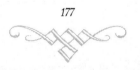

the second time, she found herself unable to look anywhere else, even unable to blink, until her eyes began to water and she was furious lest the bishop think he had moved her to tears. When he turned his attention to Lily again, she wiped surreptitiously at her eyes and dared to glance at Galen.

Appearing completely unperturbed by the bishop, who was ignoring him in turn, Galen was knitting. Rose dropped her handkerchief to her lap and watched in fascination. He was using not two, but four knitting needles, all quite short and with points at both ends. She had glimpsed him knitting a sock once out in the garden with similar needles, but those needles had been wood and much narrower. These were thicker, of softly gleaming silver that reminded her of something she couldn't quite put her finger on. Even more fascinating was *what* he was knitting: he was making a chain out of black wool. She counted eight links so far, all neatly interlocked.

He saw her looking and smiled, and she raised her eyebrows, trying to ask what on earth a wool chain was for. He just smiled even broader and cast on the stitches for a new link. Nine.

"Are you listening to me, girl!" Angier roared.

Whipping around to focus on the bishop again, Rose saw some spittle fly from the bishop's mouth and land on the back of Iris's hand. Her younger sister quickly scrubbed at it with a handkerchief, a disgusted look on her face.

"Thank you, Bishop Angier, for that rousing sermon," King Gregor said, rising to his feet. Rose could see a vein in her father's temple pulsing, as though he were on the verge of

shouting back at the bishop. "I'm sure we all feel invigorated by your words." He reached over and grabbed the bellpull, giving it a firm yank. "Let us ponder your message while we eat." He sat back down and patted Rose's hand.

The meal was a silent one, but Rose didn't know if her sisters were pondering the bishop's words any more than she was. Violet, at least, was simmering with resentment, a fact that was clear for all to see. But Hyacinth was the one who worried Rose the most. She neither spoke nor ate, and her eyes looked glassy.

Barely tasting her dinner, Rose wondered what would happen if she confessed to being a witch. Would they set Anne free, or would she still be accused of teaching Rose magic? If nothing else, it would lift the Interdict and clear the rest of her family, as long as she could convince them that she had acted alone. She would be excommunicated by the church, and likely imprisoned for life, but her father and her sisters would be free.

The only flaw was that the other girls' shoes would continue to wear out after she was gone. That, and what *he* might do if she was lost to the Midnight Ball and his eldest son.

Rose shivered. She hoped that her mother, despite her foolish bargains, had been permitted into Heaven and was too busy singing, or whatever one did there, to see the mess she had made of things. The King Under Stone had manipulated Maude from the very beginning, using her to bear twelve brides for his stern, handsome sons and then dancing her into an early grave so that her daughters would be forced to take over the contract.

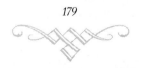

Maude hadn't suspected this, or at least, there was no indication of it in her journals. The only mention they could find of Under Stone at all was a single entry, after Orchid's birth. Maude had wondered if the potion "he" had given her had gone bad, or if she hadn't drunk it at the right time, when she bore daughter after daughter with no sign of a longed-for heir.

Rose wished that there was some way she could help Galen. If only she could leave the door in the carpet open . . . but he was asleep and could not follow them even if it were possible. She thought of bringing him back some token from the underworld, but how would she make him understand what it was?

Rose drew in a breath. A token. The sound of a branch snapping. The strange silver knitting needles that Galen had been using to make, of all things, a chain. . . . She stared across the table at him, flicking her eyes down to the chain where it lay on the table beside his plate and back up again. He caught her gaze and held it.

After dinner, Lily asked Galen to play chess with her, but he began yawning as soon as they sat down to their game. A few minutes later he forfeited, begged Lily's pardon, and stretched out on a sofa to "take a little rest." Rose watched him carefully, but he seemed to be fast asleep.

"Do you think he's faking?" she asked Lily as they prepared for the Midnight Ball.

"Impossible," Lily said. "How could he be? The enchantment is too strong for anyone to resist."

Again Rose let Lily take the lamp and go first down the

golden stairs, chivvying the other girls ahead of her into the darkness and waiting as long as possible to follow. The sofa Galen slept on faced the windows, though, so she couldn't actually see him from her position in the middle of the floor. Her ears pricked up, a strange sensation, when she thought she heard a rustling noise. She took a step back from the stairs, craning to see over the back of the sofa.

"What are you doing?" Iris reached up out of the darkness and grabbed the hem of Rose's gown just as Rose started toward the sofa. "Come along, or we'll be late!"

Annoyed, Rose went down the stairs, looking over her shoulder all the way. She tripped twice and snagged her hem on the edge of a step as she went, but she didn't care. She could have sworn that she heard booted feet crossing the room. But when the golden stair ascended behind them, there was no sign of Galen.

Goblet

Galen laughed silently to himself all the way down the golden steps. Clever Rose! She clearly suspected something. He had seen the look on her face at dinner, as though a light were dawning, and was disappointed when she didn't pull him aside to question him. Still, it was better this way. He didn't want to raise her hopes when he still had no idea how much help he could be.

Galen paused to study the silver gate after the princesses had passed through. He noticed that, although there was no fence connected to the gate, there was still a definite boundary running as far as he could see in either direction. On the staircase side of the gate, the ground did not feel like dirt or pavement, it simply felt . . . like nothing. It was neither hard nor soft, neither rough nor smooth. It was simply nothing, and then, as sharply as though someone had drawn a line with a knife, the forest began, with its sparkling black dirt and silver trees.

Nodding to himself, Galen stepped through the gate and

let it swing shut behind him. Rose whirled around and squinted, but again Iris tugged at her and she had to follow.

Through the silver forest they went, to the shore of the black lake. Again Galen hopped aboard the golden boat with Rose and her suitor, and again her suitor struggled to keep up. He kept shooting glances at Rose's figure in the bow, however, and Galen wondered if he were trying to determine if she had gained weight or not.

Galen thought Rose had never looked lovelier. Of course, he had seen her only once before her illness, and that time she had been dripping wet. But she was fully recovered now: her cheeks glowed with health rather than fever, and she no longer looked as gaunt as she had. She was wearing her red velvet gown, and over her elbows she had draped the white shawl he had made her. He thought it set off her gown and her golden-brown hair admirably.

As soon as the bottom of the boat grated on the beach, Galen jumped out, and Rose's dark escort nearly fell as he hauled it up the sand. He had overcompensated, clearly expecting the boat to be heavier. Galen, a little disappointed that his rival hadn't fallen into the wet sand, sighed. Rose looked around, and he held his breath. Then her suitor captured her attention, and her arm, and they led the way toward the dark palace.

Galen had to admit that they made a fine pair. Stately, attractive, beautifully dressed. Lily and Jonquil followed, then the rest in order of age. The haughty expressions and fine clothes of the suitors toward the end of the line seemed ridiculous to Galen, considering that they were squiring girls at least half their ages.

Still, even Petunia wore a ballgown, though suitably high necked, and her hair was in loose curls rather than pinned up like her older sisters'. As Galen followed Petunia and her escort into the palace he shuddered, thinking about the king's intent to marry the princesses to his hard-faced sons. Petunia would be perhaps fourteen or fifteen when she married her prince, and that was only if the king waited until their years of servitude were finished.

The cold-eyed courtiers clapped, the princesses curtsied, and the ball began in earnest. Galen watched the dancing for a while, but then he felt thirsty. As a servant whisked by, Galen snatched a silver goblet from the man's tray and quickly concealed it within his cape. Galen carried it over to one corner where he was partially hidden by a drape and drank thirstily. Then he put the goblet, which was of strange workmanship, into the pouch at his belt. Another souvenir for King Gregor, he thought.

When Pansy begged to sit out a dance, Galen sat beside her once more. As though sensing his presence, she began looking around, even lifting her pink skirts to stare under her chair.

"Are you there, spirit?" she asked finally.

"I am here," Galen said in a hollow voice.

"Why?"

"I want to help you."

"Oh."

"Tell me, Princess, how did your mother find the King Under Stone?"

"What do you mean?"

"Did he come to her, or did she come here, to make their

bargain?" Trying to talk in a ghostly voice strained Galen's throat, and he wished for something more to drink.

"She came here," Pansy answered readily. "Rose says that's how the silver forest got made. The first time Mother came, she dropped her brooch. It was a silver cross with laurel leaves around it that her godfather gave her. The next night it grew into a forest." She grimaced. "I tried to grow a tree out of my garnet ring once, but it didn't work," she added.

"I see." Galen paused. A forest of silver that grew from a cross? No wonder the twigs he had taken felt powerful. His hands still tingled faintly from knitting with them. "Can the princes come through the gate any time they want? How do they get to the surface? Surely not by your golden staircase?"

Pansy's brow wrinkled. "No, the princes can only come at night. I don't know how, though. They came to the garden one night, when Papa locked us in our rooms. But the next night, they could barely dance. They *hate* the forest. When Rose was sick she fainted, and Prince Illiken carried her to the gate. He looked ill, too, by the time we got to the stairs. Petunia threw up that night, and Lily had to carry her all the way from the boats. Petunia's partner, Prince Kestilan, didn't want to do it because she smelled nasty." Pansy giggled.

Galen laughed with her, choking it off when Rose and Lily and their suitors came over to the chairs. They all smiled vaguely at Pansy.

"What's so funny, Pan?" Rose smoothed Pansy's tousled curls. "Who have you been talking to?"

Galen leaned close to Pansy's ear and whispered; "Ssshhh," as quietly as he could.

"No one," Pansy said, slipping off her chair. "I know; I have to keep dancing." And she went off to find her suitor in better spirits than Galen had ever seen her.

"What's gotten into her?" Lily mused.

"I don't know," Rose said, thoughtful.

She looked right at the spot where Galen was sitting, and he felt a chill run up his arms. Even though she was looking through him, he sensed that she knew he was there. He reached out a tentative finger and touched the back of her hand. Her fingers twitched, but she did not jump or cry out; instead a small smile curved her mouth.

"We must dance," Prince Illiken said, and he led her away.

"One more night," Galen whispered when they had gone away. "One more night, and then I will get you out of this place. And your sisters, too."

Galen watched the rest of the ball without speaking, although several times both Rose and Pansy tried to linger near the chairs where he sat. He rode in Lily's boat as they went back across the lake, Galen's added weight confusing her suitor and giving Rose's Illiken an undeserved respite.

Again, Galen slipped up the stairs before the princesses without making a sound. When Rose checked to see if he was sleeping, he was snoring peacefully, inhaling the scent of her perfume as she leaned over the back of the sofa.

Governess

Galen awoke feeling confident, but that began to fade soon after breakfast. He had made a chain out of the crone's black wool that was long enough to wrap around the handles of the gate, but would it do the job? The crone's cloak really did render him invisible, and he had knitted the black wool chain with the twigs of the silver trees, his hands tingling with dormant power. But was this the answer? Would it really stop the King Under Stone from getting what he wanted?

Galen had made Rose's shawl out of the crone's white wool, thinking that it would somehow protect and comfort her, but it had no effect on Illiken when he danced with Rose. Now he worried that his instincts weren't correct.

Galen went out to the gardens that afternoon, looking for Walter, but he couldn't find the old man. He was in need of advice but didn't know where to go.

Galen stood at the entrance of the hedge maze and stared up at the palace. The pink stucco was cheery, despite the lowering clouds and threat of snow. Galen shook his head over all the nights wasted patrolling the garden, when all along the princesses were using a secret passage in their own sitting room. He frowned. Who had set up the secret passage? The King Under Stone or Queen Maude? If the princesses knew, they couldn't say.

But there was someone else in the palace who might know.

The Bretoner governess was being kept in one of garret rooms where the lowliest scullery maids slept. She had both a priest and a palace guard watching her door, and no one was allowed to speak to her without Bishop Angier present. Galen thought about using his letter from King Gregor to see her, but it gave him the freedom of the grounds only, not the palace, and certainly not the right to speak to a prisoner under Bishop Angier's care.

So he fastened on the cloak and went around to the back of the palace. The building was modern and square, and there were copper drainpipes at all the corners. Galen shimmied up the one at the western corner, closest to Anne's room. When he was level with the garret windows, he reached across, catching a window frame with one foot and his hand. Heart thumping, afraid to look down, he let go of the drainpipe and half leaped onto the narrow window ledge.

He strained at the window, which was latched from the inside, and saw a white face peering out, looking for the source of the small scraping noises he had made. The governess's eyes were puffy from crying, and her graying hair was tangled.

Galen unhooked the chain of the cloak, and the governess

let out a small scream as he appeared right in front of her. He held a finger to his lips and smiled to show that he was friendly.

"I want to help," he mouthed broadly.

She didn't look entirely convinced, but she unlatched the window and opened it a crack. "Who are you?"

"I'm Galen Werner, a gardener," he told her. "Please let me in. I need to ask you some questions."

"I've been asked enough questions," she said, and made as if to close the window again.

"Please," Galen begged. "I'm only trying to help."

She hesitated, then opened the window a little more. Galen grabbed the edge and slid it all the way open, tumbling forward into the room.

The tiny chamber contained only a cot, a table, and a chair. There were no books or sewing to occupy the governess's empty hours; there wasn't even a basin to wash her face.

"How did you— You just appeared— Who sent you?" Anne backed away from Galen, looking wary. But she kept her voice down, all the same, so that her guards would not hear them.

"My name is Galen; I work in the garden. I'm trying to help the girls . . . the princesses," Galen amended. "I followed them last night, using this." He refastened the cloak and disappeared.

Anne gasped and put her hands to her mouth, and Galen quickly took off the cloak.

"A kindly old woman gave it to me," he told her. "Along

with the wool I used for this." He pulled the black chain out of the pouch at his belt. "I want to seal the entrance to the underground realm where they dance at night. There is a gate the princesses must pass through...." His voice trailed off. The idea seemed so foolish now. "Do you know anything that would help?"

Fingering the chain, Anne shook her head, and Galen's heart sank. It was true: she was completely innocent of her charges' midnight activities.

But her next words turned Galen's pity for her imprisonment to anger.

"This feels so flimsy. I don't know that it will be enough to hold Under Stone," she said.

"You know about the King Under Stone?" Galen barely kept his voice under control. "Why didn't you tell someone? Why didn't you help them?"

"I only just discovered what Maude had done," Anne told him hastily. She sat on her narrow cot and pulled the boiled wool blanket around her plump shoulders. "And I wasn't about to tell that awful Bishop Angier.

"I was Maude's friend, her only confidant, for many years," she continued, "yet she did not confide this in me. I knew that she'd done *something*, but I thought that she'd merely found some witch to provide her with a fertility charm. She visited them all, you know. Every midwife, wisewoman, white witch, fortune-teller ... She drank horrible concoctions, ate nothing but boiled eggs one week, grapes another; had the maids wash her clothing in rainwater and dry it under the full moon...."

Anne shook her head. "None of it worked. And then Maude stopped talking to me, stopped sharing her secrets with me, and Rose was born. Rose, and the rest of the girls. Twelve children in eleven years would wear anyone out, but I always felt in my heart that something more was weighing on poor Maude. And when she died, and the girls began to look exhausted all the time, when they wore out their shoes every third night, I knew that whatever Maude had done to have her daughters was still being paid for.

"I searched the entire palace over and over again, even the rooms up here." She gestured around at the bare cell. "I only just found the books, hours before Angier came. He caught me with them. I never had a chance to do more than glance at them."

"Which books?" Galen had to clear his throat before he could ask. He had been leaning forward, listening to her tumbled words, and had forgotten to swallow.

"A history, moldy with age, that told the story of Under Stone and how he was cast down. And a diary of Maude's, detailing her dealings with him. They were hidden in the library. I only found them because I dropped a pencil, and it rolled behind one of the bookcases. The books were wedged there."

"What were you able to read?"

"Only that Maude made two bargains with him: one for her children, and one to end the war with Analousia. And something in the history, about the magicians who survived the imprisoning spell. They're not dead." She shook her head. "I didn't have enough time to make sense of it," she said, frustrated.

"Where are the books now?"

"In Angier's chambers, as far as I know," Anne said. "But how will you get to them?"

"Easily." Galen refastened his cloak and turned invisible. He felt a smile spreading across his face. The answers were waiting; all he had to do was snatch them. "Easily."

He went to the window and swung himself out and down the drainpipe. "Good luck to you," he called softly back to Anne.

"And to you," she answered, but there was still great doubt in her voice.

Third Night

Hurrying through the palace corridors, still invisible, Galen knew what the crone had been cackling about when she said that the cloak was dangerous. Dodging the maids was bad enough, but one of the footmen pulled a rug right out from under his feet, taking it up to be aired. A door was nearly slammed on his hand, and he had to pause and compose himself outside Angier's door.

Galen listened at the keyhole but didn't hear anything, so he picked the lock with a penknife and entered the rooms. A quick search showed that the sitting room and adjoining bed-chamber were indeed empty, and Galen turned his attention to finding the books Anne had described.

It didn't take long to locate them.

Bishop Angier, confident that no one would dare to rifle through his things, had simply left them on a table. There were other books: a notebook in Analousian that Galen guessed was the bishop's, a book on the history of witchcraft, and a beautifully illustrated Bible.

Galen pushed these other books aside, picking up the tattered history book and the small blue diary that also littered the table. He started to put them in his satchel, but then realized that when their absence was discovered, it might raise a hue and cry.

Galen set them back on the table and began hastily leafing through the history, to see what he could find before Angier returned. Halfway through the book, he found a pansy pressed between two pages. Maude had used the flower to mark the chapter on Under Stone.

Galen sank onto the edge of the table and read about the King Under Stone, whose name had once been Wolfram von Aue, when he was an adviser to King Ranulf of Westfalin in the fifth century. When he killed Ranulf and made himself king, Under Stone had decreed that his name must never be spoken again, lest it be used against him as part of a spell. Every record, every piece of paper that contained his name had been destroyed, and the very memory of it had been wiped from the minds of his subjects. The magicians who imprisoned him had spent years trying to recover that name, which was the key to their spell of entrapment. It had also involved silver, blessed by a bishop, and wool from a lamb that had never before been sheared.

Galen reached into his satchel and stroked the woolen chain. He felt sure that this wool had come from a similar source. Who had that old woman been?

The answer was found at the end of the chapter. Twelve magicians had imprisoned the King Under Stone, as he was now called. Eight of them had died, but four remained alive, and more than that.

> *Never certain if a being so powerful and so wicked could truly be defeated, the four living magicians took upon themselves immortality, to walk the world until the end of time. Though diminished in strength, they are ever guarding against the dark king and those like him, lest they return to the world and cause more mischief.*

Those like him? Galen shuddered at the thought that there might be other creatures like Under Stone out there.

He turned to Maude's diary, feeling a bit embarrassed at perusing the private thoughts of a queen. Here Angier helped him: a bookmark of purple satin with the bishop's seal embroidered on it had been placed in the pertinent part of the book. Maude had learned of Under Stone not only from the old history she found, but from one of the magicians she had consulted in her hunger to have a baby.

The "goodwife," as Maude called her, had told the queen how Under Stone had managed to summon mortal princesses to him in order to father his twelve sons, which is where Maude got the idea that he might help her as well. The goodwife, though Galen wouldn't have called her that, told Maude how to call to the king by placing a drop of blood on a white silk handkerchief, pressing it to the ground under a new moon,

and calling his true name. Maude had done it at the far end of the garden, near an old oak tree that was one of the few original trees that had been left standing when King Gregor remade the garden for his bride. Galen wondered if that was also where Rionin and his brothers had entered the gardens.

She had made the bargain with the King Under Stone, only wanting one child, but the king had "graciously" promised her a dozen. Her original entries about her dealings with him had been elated; she had only to come to his palace and dance when the moon was full. Then Rose was born the day of the full moon, and Maude had not gone to dance. When next she went down the golden staircase, the King Under Stone had raged at her and told her to come twice a month. With every missed ball, he increased the number, until she was dancing every third night until the week she died. By the end her handwriting was jagged with despair, and tears had made the ink run. She hadn't really wanted to make the bargain to end the war, but she could think of no other way to help her beloved Gregor, and Under Stone had been kinder of late. . . .

Galen read it all in horror, able to see what Maude could not, that Under Stone had manipulated and used her, playing off her dreams of children, of peace, promising her everything and asking so very little.

Only that she dance for him, to give him power.

Only that she bear twelve daughters, who would one day marry his sons.

That was never mentioned in the bargain, of course. Galen

closed the diary with an oath. He replaced the book carefully where he had found it—on top of the history, at an angle—and went quickly across the sitting room to the door. But when he put a hand on the knob, he heard voices in the corridor and stepped back.

The door swung open, and Angier entered with his assistant, Father Michel. And Petunia.

Rather than slipping out before the junior priest could close the door, Galen remained, pressed up against the wall. Petunia looked frightened, and the bishop was holding her tightly by the upper arm. He sat her down in a chair and stood over her. Galen hardly dared to breathe.

The bishop didn't engage in any pleasantries but got straight to the important question: "Where do you and your sisters go every night?"

Petunia didn't say anything; she just shook her head.

"You won't tell me, or you don't know?"

Another head shake.

"Do you want to be put in a dungeon, and your sisters, too?" Angier's question made Galen grit his teeth.

"N-no," came Petunia's piping voice. "We want to stay here with Papa."

"Then tell me where you go every night!"

"I can't," the child wailed.

"You can and you will. Who is responsible for the princes' deaths? The Bretoner woman? Your father? Your older sisters? Tell me!"

Galen clenched his hands into fists. Had King Gregor really given permission for his youngest daughter to be interrogated like a criminal?

Looking frantically around the room, Galen tried to think of something, anything he could do to stop this, as the bishop's questions went on and on and Petunia began to sob. He couldn't attack a bishop, and if he opened the door and went to see King Gregor, they would notice.

Just as Galen was thinking the risk was worth it, and hoping that they would only think the palace haunted when the door swung open, someone came stomping down the hallway and pounded on the door. The other priest opened it to reveal a red-faced King Gregor with Rose, Lily, and Bishop Schelker standing behind him.

Petunia leaped to her feet and raced across the room to bury her face in Rose's skirt.

"Your Excellency," the king said with barely controlled rage. "I gave permission for my older daughters to be questioned, but not the younger set. And none of them were to be questioned alone, without even a maid there to provide support."

"I need to get to the bottom of this, Gregor," the bishop said, his voice cold. "The governess and your older daughters will not talk; I thought perhaps the younger ones would be innocent enough not to lie."

"My daughters are not liars," King Gregor said through clenched teeth. "If there is witchcraft afoot, then they are its victims, and you should show them compassion."

"This is very much against policy, Brother Angier," Bishop Schelker added.

Behind Rose, the door was still open, and as Galen knew that Petunia had more protection than he could rightly offer, he slipped out. Rose looked around, startled, as he accidentally brushed against her, and he held his breath for a moment as she peered right through him.

"You may continue to question her, however," King Gregor was saying as he shut the door. "You may question us all, in fact. Together."

Out in the hallway, Galen breathed a sigh of relief. He took off his cloak and pushed it into his satchel, tired of creeping around and nearly being stepped on. Turning over in his mind all the information he had just read, Galen's thoughts strayed to the governess, sitting on her bed and fingering the flimsy wool chain, her blanket wrapped around her shoulders.

The blanket had been dark green boiled wool, something Galen was very familiar with. Army blankets were made of the same stuff, and in a pinch you could use them to make a lean-to, or to line the inside of a boot that was wearing out. Boiled wool was itchy and stiff, and soldiers joked that it was bulletproof, so that no one could shoot you in your sleep.

Bulletproof? Perhaps not. But stronger than regular wool? Yes.

He went to the kitchens and asked to speak to the head cook. She was a large woman, with the air of someone usually good-tempered who was having a bad day. She shouted at the

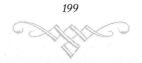

staff, but halfheartedly, and they all spooked and scrambled whenever she did, as though uneasy themselves.

"My dear goodfrau," Galen said warmly. "I am Galen Werner; I've been a guest here the past two nights. Please let me compliment you on your cooking."

"You're the young gardener," she grunted. Then she flipped two cookies off a tray with a spatula and waved at Galen to take them.

"I am. And so I assume you know why I'm now a guest in the palace?" He glanced around, not wanting to let the entire kitchen in on his plan.

"I do," the cook said in a low voice. "I'm guessing you want some help?"

"If you would be so kind . . . ?"

"Not sure what I can do," she said with a shrug.

"Something very simple." He fished out the black wool chain. "I'd like you to boil this. With this, and this." He took the basil from his pocket and the nightshade from under his lapel and laid all three items on the table.

The plump cook's mouth fell open. "You want me to boil these? Together?"

"Yes, if you would be so kind."

"But why?"

"I'm afraid I can't tell you," Galen said. "But if you could just keep it all in a pot, covered and boiling, tonight, I would pay you." He thought of his meager collection of coins, and figured that it would be enough for so simple a task.

"And this will help the princesses?"

"I hope so."

"All right," the woman said doubtfully. "I'll do it. But you don't need to pay me."

"Thank you."

⚭

Feeling like he was gaining an advantage at last, Galen picked more basil and nightshade for his pockets, and was in almost buoyant good spirits during Bishop Angier's evening sermon. Supported by her father and eldest sisters, Petunia had emerged from the bishop's chambers with a tear-stained face but her exuberant nature only slightly dampened.

After dinner Galen played cards with Violet, Iris, and Orchid. He forced himself to yawn several times but didn't pretend to fall asleep until after Violet had defeated them all.

Sand

Back on the sofa where Galen had "slept" the night before, he snored his best while the girls prepared themselves for the ball. At one point, he caught himself starting to fall asleep in truth. Fishing a knitting needle from his satchel with one hand, he jabbed himself in the leg with it every time he began to doze. Then, concealed by the back of the sofa, he slipped on his purple cape and was hard on Rose's heels as soon as the staircase began to lower.

As they descended the golden stair, the white shawl slipped from Rose's shoulders and without thinking he gently lifted it back into place.

"Thank you," she said. Then she stopped dead and looked over her shoulder with a half-fearful, half-hopeful expression. "Galen?"

"Rose? What is it?" Pansy came and took her eldest sister's hand as the others continued on down the steps.

"Nothing." Rose shook her head as though to clear it. "I

keep thinking— Never mind." Leading Pansy by the hand, Rose continued on down the stairs.

"Was it the good spirit?"

This made Rose stop again. "What did you say?"

"I've been talking to a good spirit at the ball the last two nights," Pansy confided, her little face turned up adoringly to her sister's. "He's very kind. He cheers me up when I am tired and sad."

"He—he does?"

"Rose! Pansy!" Jonquil, standing with the other princesses at the foot of the staircase, looked up with an irritated expression. "Why are you two dawdling up there?"

"We're coming." Rose hurried Pansy down the rest of the stairs. "Who does the spirit sound like?" she whispered as they went.

"A spirit," Pansy said; then she clapped a hand to her mouth. "I'm not supposed to talk about it," she said from between her fingers. "It's a secret."

To Galen's relief, they reached the silver and pearl gate before Rose could convince Pansy to tell her any more. He rode in the boat with Jonquil and her prince, who was not as stoic as his brothers.

"What did you eat for dinner?" the dark prince huffed.

"What do you mean?" Jonquil frowned at her escort as he rowed.

"You're so heavy, it's like you're wearing iron underthings," he panted.

"Oh!" Jonquil whacked her prince on the shoulder with her fan. "How rude!"

When their boat reached the island and the black palace, Jonquil leaped out without waiting for assistance. She stalked into the palace ahead of everyone else, with her prince scuttling at her heels, apologizing every step of the way. Laughing to himself, Galen lagged behind to scoop up some of the coarse black sand. He tied it into his handkerchief and then stuffed the bundle into his belt pouch.

Thirsty, Galen helped himself to a goblet when they reached the ballroom. He noticed that Rose was still on the alert, searching the corners of the room for any sign of something unusual. Prince Illiken tried to regain her attention by holding even more tightly to her narrow waist, which made Galen reach for another goblet, and another. Finally Illiken grew so impatient with her distracted air that he stalked off to get his own drink, leaving Rose near the chairs where Galen played "good spirit" with Pansy.

Galen stowed the goblets behind a curtain and walked up to twitch the hem of Rose's shawl. She gasped and looked around.

"Hello," Galen said in a low voice. "Would you like to dance?"

"So you're Pansy's good spirit?"

"I am."

"Your voice sounds familiar." Her eyes sparkled. "Could you pretend to snore, so that I could make sure?"

Galen didn't answer. He caught Rose around the waist and

spun her out onto the dance floor. She held her arms wide and laughed, letting Galen lead her in circles around the other dancers. They stared at the princess as she danced wildly across the gleaming floor. They could not see Galen, and as they passed Lily he heard her gasp that Rose was acting mad. Rose heard too, and laughed harder.

Galen leaned close to her ear. "Could the king come aboveground?"

The question sobered Rose but couldn't keep the sparkle out of her eyes. "No. The king cannot leave here, ever."

"I can seal the gate in the morning," Galen told her. "You will never have to dance again!"

"The stairs will not work until midnight," Rose said, shaking her head as he spun her around. Pins flew from her elaborate coiffure and clattered across the floor.

"Don't worry, I will set you free," Galen said, becoming bold. "Rose, I—"

"What is this?" Unannounced, the pale King Under Stone slammed into the ballroom and stood glaring at the giddy Rose. Belatedly the trumpeters began to blow a fanfare, but the king cut them off with a sharp gesture.

Rose stepped away from Galen and curtsied unsteadily. "Please forgive me, Your Majesty. I . . . became intoxicated with the music."

Prince Illiken arrived at her side, his pale face scarlet with embarrassment. Rose pretended to lean against him as though exhausted, and Galen strangled his jealousy.

"I see." But now the king frowned around the room

suspiciously. As his eyes passed over the place where Galen stood, they hesitated for the barest instant, and Galen felt sweat roll down his cheeks and back. "Come here, dear Rose," the king said, beckoning to her. "The rest of you, continue dancing."

The musicians took up their instruments again, and the other dancers once more moved across the floor. Prince Illiken at her elbow, Rose stood at the foot of the dais and faced the king.

"I understand that you have yet another young man sniffing at your skirts," the cold king said.

"I don't know what you mean," Rose said stiffly. "Your Majesty."

"Don't lie to me, Rose. I may be trapped down here, but I am not unaware of what goes on up there." He pointed one skeletal finger skyward.

"There is a young man at the palace right now," Rose said reluctantly. "But he's only a commoner." Her voice became dismissive. "One of the gardeners, if you can believe it!" She laughed, and humiliation washed over Galen, but then he looked at her face and saw the rigidity of her expression and the hint of moisture in her eyes. She was sweating a little with the strain of maintaining the charade in front of the king.

"But then, all of your daylight-dwelling suitors have been common, compared to my sons. Does this gardener hope for the ultimate reward?" A smile slit the king's face. "To marry a beautiful princess?" A chilling laugh.

"Your gardener should feel honored: he will not marry a princess, but he will die a princely death." Again the king laughed, and Galen felt sick.

"H-he will?" Rose swallowed loudly.

"Of course. Before the month is out he will be punished for his audacity, just as the others have been. What will it be?" the king mused. "A duel? A riding accident? It pleases me to dispatch him in the same way that I got rid of the foolish nobles. I shall have to think on it. It would be an unworthy death for one who aspired so high, to be run over by a farmer's cart."

"Why did you have to ... The princes. . . ." Rose trailed off, shivering, and pulled the white shawl closer around her shoulders, much to Galen's delight. "Excuse me, Your Majesty." She curtsied to the king and moved away from him on the arm of Prince Illiken. Galen followed them, trying not to think about how he would die.

"You mustn't anger Father," Illiken said in his wooden voice.

"I—," Rose started to say; then she just shook her head and looked away.

Prince Illiken stopped and Galen jumped back just in time to avoid treading on the back of the prince's shoe.

"Who is this commoner who courts you?" The faint curiosity was the most emotion Galen had ever heard from Illiken. Curiosity, and could it be jealousy?

"He's not courting me," Rose said, but her tone was uneasy, and something else Galen couldn't identify.

"But he searches for answers?"

"Well, yes."

"And if he succeeds, he will marry one of you?" Prince Illiken's black eyes narrowed.

"He offered to do it without the, er, reward," Rose said

defensively. "Of course, my poor father will probably give him anything he wants if he uncovers the truth." She raised her chin.

"He will not find out," Illiken said simply. "And even if he did, he could not help you." And then, without warning, he grabbed Rose and pulled her into the figures of the next dance. She stumbled, but he was holding her so tightly that she didn't fall—although it did take her several staggering steps to join in the dance properly.

"Oaf," Galen said aloud, and thought of several other things he'd like to call Illiken as well.

"What did you say?" The woman standing behind him turned to her partner in confusion.

"I didn't say anything," the man replied. As they moved off to join the dance as well, Galen blew on the woman's neck and made her shriek. He sat down in his "good spirit" chair and tried to think.

He wondered if Walter would be able to help protect him from Under Stone, if the king really did try to have him killed. Galen had his suspicions about the old gardener and who he really was. If Walter had done anything to protect the princes, though, it hadn't worked. But then, Walter hadn't particularly cared for any of them.

Galen was forced to leap up again a moment later, when someone nearly sat in his lap. The edge of his cloak caught on the white-faced courtier's hand as Galen slid away, and the man suddenly got up and walked out of the ballroom, rather than sitting down after all. Cursing softly to himself, Galen readjusted his cloak and stood in the corner until the ball ended.

By the time the princesses were allowed to leave, Pansy and Petunia were so tired that their princes had to carry them. Galen got ready to step into Jonquil's boat again, to see if her prince would again comment on the slender girl's weight.

Before any of them could push off, however, the King Under Stone came stalking out of the palace, his pale face horrible with rage. Just behind him was the man who had nearly sat on Galen.

"Halt," the king shouted. "Halt! Intruder!" In one hand he held a goblet and in the other a wilted sprig of nightshade. Lifting the incriminating items high, the king said, "The lips of a human male have touched this goblet! Nightshade has been brought into my home! *Where is he?*"

Galen felt frantically in his pockets and under his lapel. The basil was still there, but the nightshade was gone; only the pin remained.

Terrible black eyes raked over Galen, passed on, and then came back. Despite the cloak, the King Under Stone could see him, Galen was certain. A long finger pointed, the king's pale lips twisted around words that keened and chattered in Galen's ears. Dimly Galen heard the princesses screaming, felt a cold wind rush over him.

The world went dark, and in that darkness Galen clearly heard the voice of the King Under Stone: "You will die ere the moon grows full again."

Riot

Galen awakened to the sound of heavy knocking on the door to the princesses' sitting room. Groggy, he picked himself up off the floor and stumbled to the door, not comprehending when the palace guard who had been knocking looked through him, puzzled, and called out for Princess Rose.

"What's this?" Maria the head maid came out of one of the bedrooms, hair mussed and gown creased. "What's the to-do, Captain?" She stepped past Galen as if he weren't even there.

Belatedly Galen realized that he was still wearing the invisibility cloak. He would have to sneak down the hall and slip out of it in his room. He didn't want to just reappear in front of the servants, or the princesses.

The events of the last night jolted through Galen's brain. The King Under Stone had seen him. Galen would be dead before the next full moon, which was in roughly three days. And Rose . . . Galen had been asleep in the middle of the gold-patterned carpet. If the princesses had returned, they would have stumbled over him.

If the princesses had returned.

Ignoring the hurried whispers of the maid and the guard, Galen ran to the door of Rose's bedroom and peered in. The beds were neatly made, and one of their other maids was still slumped on a sofa in the corner. There was no sign of any of the princesses. Galen stepped into the room, whipped off his cloak, and came running back out with a shout.

"The princesses are gone!"

Maria and the guard stared at him in astonishment.

Galen ran to one of the other bedrooms and threw open the door. There he saw another maid, this one just starting to wake, and another row of unoccupied beds. "The princesses are gone!"

"What?" Now understanding dawned, and Maria and the guard joined him in searching the rooms. There were four maids and no princesses.

"They've been taken hostage," the guard said, crossing himself. "The mob must have broken in."

"What mob?" Galen stared at him.

"The townsfolk are rioting," the guard said.

It suddenly dawned on Galen that this must be what the man had come to the princesses' rooms to report.

"They're demanding that Fraulein Anne be hung, and the Interdict lifted." The guard looked around uncomfortably. "All this talk of witchcraft, and the princesses killing those foreign princes . . . well, and not being able to bury their dead or receive the sacred rites . . ."

But Galen shook his head, casting this information aside. None of that mattered now. The King Under Stone had Rose, and he would never let her or her sisters leave his realm again.

"I must speak to the king," Galen said urgently, rushing out of the sitting room with the other two at his heels.

Bishop Angier was with King Gregor, of course. So were the prime minister and the rest of the king's councillors, including Bishop Schelker, his brow furrowed and his eyes on Angier.

Puzzlement showed on King Gregor's face when Galen walked into the room with the guard captain and Maria. He looked beyond them to the hallway. "Master Werner, where are my daughters?"

"They are not here, Your Majesty," Galen said, bowing. He wished he did not have to explain everything in front of an audience.

"Someone has taken them hostage, sire," the captain blurted out. "This person claims he knows who."

The room erupted at the news. The ministers began to babble, waving their arms and pointing out the window. Galen craned his neck and could see a regiment of guards standing in formation in the courtyard below.

"Silence!" the king shouted. "Silence, all of you!" He stepped forward and gripped Galen's shoulder tightly. "Who has taken my girls?"

Galen took a deep breath. "The same creature who forces them to dance, night after night, Your Majesty. The King Under Stone."

The prime minister let out a bitter guffaw. "Get him out

of here, Captain," he said, gesturing to the guard beside Galen. "He's mad. Or a fool. Or both."

"Or he's in league with the rioters," said another minister. "Take him for questioning."

Galen's eyes never left the king's. In King Gregor's face, Galen could see the realization that the king knew he spoke the truth. Terror flickered in the king's eyes. Over the king's shoulder, Galen saw Bishop Schelker half rise. His face, too, showed a horror that told Galen the Bishop of Bruch knew the legends were true as well.

"You have proof," King Gregor said in a dry whisper. It was not a question.

Galen reached for the pouch at his waist, shifting aside the purple cloak he had tucked awkwardly into his belt. Hard hands closed on Galen's arms from behind.

"Don't move," the captain said in a low voice. "Your Majesty, please step away."

"Take him to my rooms," Angier said, waving his hand at the captain. "I will question him later."

"Bishop Angier, I must speak with the boy," King Gregor protested, stepping away from Galen even as the captain began to haul him backward.

"Brother Angier," Bishop Schelker began.

"I said, take him away!" Angier shouted, pounding his fist on a table.

The captain clamped down on Galen's arms and started to haul him out of the room. Galen struggled but couldn't break his grip.

"Every night the princesses descend a golden staircase in their sitting room!" Galen shouted. "They walk through a silver forest and are rowed across a black lake to a palace where they dance with twelve princes, the King Under Stone's sons! Queen Maude was tricked!" By this time they were already out in the passageway, and the door had been shut behind them.

"Shut up," the captain said, and smacked the back of Galen's head with one hand.

Galen twisted in the grip of the captain's single restraining hand and finally broke free. In one quick movement Galen whipped the invisibility cloak around himself and fastened the clasp. The captain gasped as Galen disappeared before his eyes, and Galen backed slowly away from the man, keeping to the carpeted center of the passageway so that his boots wouldn't make any noise.

Ducking into the first room he came to, he tried to shut out the shouts of the captain as he roused the rest of the household guards. Finding himself in the music room, which overlooked the front gates, Galen hastened around the pianoforte to lean over a small sofa by the window. The regiment of soldiers standing in the courtyard had not moved, and now Galen could see beyond them to the gates. It looked like the whole city of Bruch stood there, shaking their fists and chanting, "Hang the witch!"

Galen turned away and went back into the corridor. The guard was farther down the hall, opening and closing doors, looking for Galen. Galen crept past him and went down the back stairs to the kitchens. In the shadows just outside the baize kitchen door he pulled off his cloak and shoved it into his satchel.

Counting on the fact that the kitchen servants would be the last to know that he was under arrest, Galen strode in as though he hadn't a care in the world. The head cook quickly beckoned him over to the stove in the far corner, where a large black pot bubbled merrily away.

"The chain shrunk," she said in a whisper.

"It's supposed to," he assured her.

With a wooden spoon she fished out the black wool, wrapped it in a towel to wring out some of the water, and then handed the wet thing to Galen.

He fingered the links carefully. They were thicker and harder, but smaller. He couldn't poke a finger between the stitches anymore. In fact, the wool appeared solid: no stitches were in evidence. It was exactly as he had wished, even down to the sharp smell of the herbs it had been boiled with.

"My dear goodfrau, you are a gem," Galen told her. He kissed her round cheek, stuck the chain in his bag, and went out the kitchen door into the garden.

He picked himself new sprigs of basil and nightshade, for what he hoped was the last time, and then he used some ivy to climb over the garden wall. He considered putting the cloak on again, but the streets at the back of the palace were deserted.

Making his way to his uncle's house, he saw that there was mud spattered on the pink stucco, and the window boxes on the ground floor had been ripped off and thrown in the streets.

It seemed that, unable to reach the palace itself, some of the protestors had taken out their ire on the head gardener of the King's Folly.

The door was locked, and Galen had no key, so he knocked. It took a few moments for anyone to answer, but at last Uncle Reiner opened the door a crack, a suspicious look on his face. Seeing that Galen was alone, he grudgingly stood aside to let him in.

"Are you well, sir?" Galen asked. "And Tante Liesel and Ulrike?"

Reiner nodded.

"What of the other gardeners? Walter?"

"I sent word for Walter and the others to stay at home for the time being," Reiner grunted. "I had hardly gotten two steps from the door this morning when a group of rabble-rousers swept by me. Have they broken into the palace?"

"They're still outside the gates," Galen said. "But I don't know how long they'll be content to simply stand there and shake their fists."

Reiner shook his head, his face grim. "To think that it should have come to this," he muttered. "Throwing mud and rocks at *my* house, shouting obscenities at the palace . . . disgraceful!"

Ulrike came down the stairs, and her face brightened when she saw Galen. "Oh, thank heavens!" She rushed over and gave him a hug. "Please say you're back for good."

"I'm afraid I'm just here to get some things, then I'll be going back to the palace," Galen said gently.

"You'll do nothing of the kind," Uncle Reiner huffed. "You

have already humiliated me by getting yourself involved in this strangeness with the princesses, and I will let it go no further.

"You need to keep your head down and work at the tasks given you: hoeing the soil and caring for the king's garden. Forget these princesses with their odd ways."

"It isn't the king's garden, and they aren't the princesses' odd ways," Galen said quietly. "They're the queen's. The garden was for her, and all this trouble"—Galen made a sweeping gesture with his arms—"is because of her as well."

"We do not speak ill of the dead in this house, boy," Uncle Reiner warned.

"She cursed her own daughters," Galen retorted, his voice gaining heat. "Cursed them from the day they were born. I even wonder if the King Under Stone didn't *start* the war so that he could gain a firmer hold on them."

"What are you talking about?" Reiner's face had gone from angry to confused, and Ulrike was staring with her mouth open.

Galen couldn't stop, though. He hadn't slept more than a pair of hours in the past few days, and all the things he had witnessed were coming together in his head. Besides which, the shouts and screams of the mob had taken him back to his days in the war.

"The war, the dancing, the rumors of witchcraft, it all comes down to this: the King Under Stone wants Rose and her sisters for his sons, and he doesn't care how many mortals die to get them." Galen stared over Uncle Reiner's shoulder, his teeth gritted.

"Stop raving, boy," Reiner said. "Go to your room and lie

down, and when this all clears over, I'll see about letting you work with me again. Go."

Galen went, but he didn't lie down. He changed out of his suit and back into his army uniform. On a heavy belt buckled over his blue soldier's coat he wore a pair of pistols and a long knife. Another knife was concealed in his right boot. He emptied out his satchel and then repacked it with the silver needles, the goblet, and the bag of black sand. On top of that he put extra powder and shot for the pistols and his rifle.

He put on the satchel, making sure that it didn't interfere with the pistols. Then he shouldered his rifle and swung the cape over it all. Invisible again, he went down the stairs and along the front hall. As he passed the sitting room, he could hear the rumble of Reiner's voice and caught his own name.

"He's gotten himself into trouble, Liesel," Reiner was saying. "If he wasn't family—"

"But he is," came Tante Liesel's fluting voice. "And we have to help him."

"Who said he was in trouble? He's just trying to help his friends." That was Ulrike.

"You don't understand," Reiner said. "It's Heinrich all over again. Galen and the eldest princess—"

But Galen didn't wait to hear any more. There was nothing he could say that would convince Reiner that Rose was innocent, and that Galen was just trying to help her. The only thing to do was to stop this and free the princesses of their curse. Galen slipped out the front door and made his way down the street.

Angier

From the gardens, all at the palace appeared to be in order. There was no sign of the mob, or anyone else for that matter. Galen hoped to see Walter come stumping down one of the paths with a wheelbarrow, whistling a jaunty tune. But the old man appeared to have taken Reiner's advice and stayed home.

Galen stowed his cape and went through the kitchen door, with a nod and a smile for the head cook, then up the stairs to the princesses' sitting room. If the rug truly wouldn't turn into a stair during the day, he was going to seek out Walter at his home.

There was a guard blocking the sitting room door.

Galen stuffed his hands in his pockets, hiding the pistols at his hips. "Mind if I go in and have a look around?"

"No one is allowed in," the guard said, staring at Galen's musket and uniform.

"The princesses haven't returned, have they?" Galen didn't

think this likely, but he wanted to know why someone was guarding an empty room.

"No, they have not," the man said, and a touch of concern colored his voice. "Look, young gardener . . . or whatever you are: just be on your way. There's nothing you can do here."

"All right," Galen said, showing reluctance. He went back out through the kitchens, and then to the south side of the palace. Putting on his cloak yet again, he carefully climbed the ivy trellis and made his way into the sitting room through an unlatched window.

Where he found Bishop Angier spreading out the princesses' jewelry on the card table. The scraping of Galen's boots on the windowsill, and the thump he made as he landed on the floor, made the bishop look up.

Directly at Galen.

"Ah, the soldier-turned-gardener. I should have known," the bishop said.

Shocked, Galen froze.

Even more bizarre, the bishop drew a pistol from his robes and aimed it at Galen's heart. "Please take it off."

Seeing Galen's consternation, Bishop Angier held up his left hand to display a large ring set with a deep purple stone. He smiled at Galen. "A witch-hunter's tools are many and varied. For instance, amethyst enables me to see through enchantment. I haven't bothered with it before now, though. The princesses seemed more stubborn than clever. But you, with your foolish grin and your endlessly clicking knitting needles, I knew that you could not possibly be as dim as you appear."

"Oh," Galen said. It was all he could think to say.

"Your cloak," Angier reminded him. "I'd like to be able to look you in the eyes more comfortably."

Galen took it off and draped it over one arm.

"Come along," Angier said.

Galen went where he was ordered: down the hall, past the startled guard who Galen now realized was there to keep the bishop from being interrupted, and into the bishop's rooms. Angier motioned Galen to a chair and then sat across from him, his pistol still at the ready.

The sitting room looked out on the front gardens, where the mob had been when Galen had left earlier. There was no sound of shouts now, however, and Galen strained to see outside without rising from his chair.

"You need have no fear of the mob," Angier said, following Galen's gaze. "I took care of them."

Galen felt a lurch of distrust. "How?"

"I assured them that the witch would hang tomorrow morning, and that the Interdict would be lifted as soon as I was satisfied that there was no further taint on the royal house," the bishop said coolly. "I promised to lead next Sunday's first mass myself." He smiled. "A week should give the king plenty of time to abdicate, don't you think?"

"Abdicate?" Galen felt cold. "But the king is innocent! And so is Fraulein Anne!"

"Of course she is," Angier said, lifting one shoulder in a shrug. "But we can't very well hang dead Queen Maude, now, can we? And the king's abdication will be a blow, I'm sure, but

the people will come to see the wisdom of it in time. The entire royal family is tainted by this witchcraft and vastly unfit to rule an otherwise godly nation like Westfalin."

Galen's thoughts roiled. Angier wasn't lying: the bishop was going to execute Anne and put pressure on King Gregor until he gave up his throne. Galen swallowed the bile that rose in his throat, and concentrated on the pistol pointed at him. He had to get out of here, and soon. It was already past noon, and Galen had no idea what Rose was going through in the kingdom Under Stone.

"Your Excellency," Galen said as calmly as he could. "Please, I only want to help the princesses."

"Help? With your filthy magic cape? You are probably the one who is hiding them from me!"

Galen decided to lay his cards on the table. He needed the bishop to be on their side. "No, Your Excellency! I swear I don't know any magic. I am only trying to save the princesses from the King Under Stone. I was given this cloak by one of the magicians who imprisoned him."

"The King Under Stone!" Angier snorted. "A fairy tale used by nasty little witches to cover up their own evil machinations. There never was a King Under Stone, boy. It's nothing but lies."

"Then who did Maude make the bargain with?" Galen pointed at the diary on the table with his chin.

A mistake. The bishop swelled like a bullfrog.

"You've been trespassing with your little cape, I see," he hissed. "Now, tell me where the princesses are!"

"I told you: they are in the prison-realm of the King Under Stone!"

"Liar!" Angier howled.

"You have the proof right there, in Queen Maude's own diaries," Galen said heatedly. "You must help me free them!"

"Abominations and lies!" Angier shook his head, jowls quivering. "You will hang for your witchcraft, boy, even if we can't prove that you abducted those poor misguided young women."

"I never would have hurt them," Galen said hotly. "I've been trying to gather information so that I could help. I came here yesterday—" Galen stopped as the bishop looked beyond him.

"Thank you, Captain, we're done," Angier said, lowering the pistol.

Galen lurched to his feet, one hand on the pistol at his belt, spinning around to see . . . nothing. There was no one behind him.

"Stupid boy." Angier laughed.

And then Galen's head exploded with pain as the bishop hit him squarely in the back of the skull with the butt of his pistol. Galen fell facedown on the lush red carpet. Through the cotton that seemed to be wrapped around his head, Galen heard Angier calling out for help, that the mad gardener had just attacked him.

Then darkness rolled up and Galen was lost.

Prisoner

Rose and her sisters had never been past the ballroom in the Palace Under Stone. Even the retiring room set aside for them with chamber pots and wash basins was immediately off the main hall, making it unnecessary for them to venture far from the ballroom. Now, however, they were deep within the palace, and Rose had decided that the bedchambers were hardly any more cozy and welcoming than the ballroom.

Everything was black. Or dark purple. Or midnight blue. There were occasional flashes of silver: the lamps, some silver gilt on a few of the chairs. But other than that, everything was dark, the colors of shadows and spiders and twilight. Their own clothes had been taken away, and they had been given wardrobes of ballgowns, morning gowns, and nightrobes in shades of black, purple, and indigo blue.

"I want my pink dress," Pansy sobbed. She had been so exhausted the night before that she hadn't protested when Lily, dismissing the strange, silent maids, had put Pansy in a filmy black nightrobe and tucked her into the ebony-wood bed. But now it was morning, although there was no sun to shine here, and Pansy was refusing to put on any of the dresses provided.

"I don't want to wear mine either," Petunia said, struggling free of Jonquil, who was trying to dress her in a dark purple gown. "It's ugly and it smells funny. Where's my yellow dress?"

Rose could hardly blame them. The clothing did indeed smell funny—like stone and earth and something else unpleasant. And the fabrics were cold and slippery and strange. She had had to repress a shudder of revulsion at the sensation of her own indigo-colored gown sliding over her head and down around her shoulders.

Her one comfort was the shawl Galen had made for her. The silent servants had tried to take that as well, but Rose had hissed at them that if they took her shawl, she would have them all beheaded. Something in her face convinced them, or perhaps it was not an unheard-of punishment for the King Under Stone's servants, for they left the shawl alone.

Her sisters had not been as fierce, or as fortunate.

"These shoes don't fit," Lilac complained, holding up a pair of black leather slippers.

"Then try some of Iris's," Rose snapped. She caught Petunia as the youngest girl tried to crawl under a bed, and held her out at arms' length while Jonquil attempted to slip the purple dress over the girl's head.

"Herr Schmidt's slippers fit us much better," Orchid announced.

225

"Of course they do; he made hundreds of them for us," Lilac said.

"Hold still," Rose shouted at Petunia. "Your yellow dress is gone; you have to wear this one!"

Her sisters all froze and stared at her. Rose never shouted.

"Listen to me," she said, doing her best to moderate her tone but sounding angry all the same. "It doesn't matter if the clothes smell funny or don't fit right. We'll get used to it soon enough. Don't you all understand? We'll never leave this place again! We'll never see the sun, never see Mother's garden, never see *Father*, ever again."

She released Petunia, half-dressed in the purple gown, and walked away. She didn't know where she was going until she had gone out the door and into the long corridor beyond. It was empty and horribly silent. Rose kept on walking.

Eventually she came to a door that was not closed. Beyond it she could see a room that mirrored the one she had left: long and narrow, with twelve tall beds. Illiken and his brothers were sitting on the various sofas, playing music on strange, shrill instruments, reading books, or simply sitting and staring.

Rose went in.

The princes all stared at her, then scrambled to their feet as one. Illiken came forward after some nudging from his brothers.

"Rose, what are you doing here? Shouldn't you be in your room?"

"Does it matter?"

"Father doesn't like it if people wander around without permission."

"None of you are very bright, are you?"

A spark of something lit in Illiken's eyes at her harsh words. "Father doesn't like us to be too clever," he said carefully, as though testing to see if she understood. "He does not appreciate rivalry."

"Nor will *you*," the King Under Stone said as he swept into the room. "If you ever sit on my throne."

Illiken's pale skin turned a sickly green, and he and his brothers bowed.

Rose remained stiffly upright, however. She was through paying homage to this evil creature.

"Where is Galen?" She had many questions to ask the king, and it surprised her a little that this should be the first one to pop out of her mouth. Still, it was just as urgent as any of the others. "What have you done to him?"

"Nothing." The king spread his weirdly elongated hands in an innocent gesture. "The gardener's boy is in perfect health. For the present."

"And then he'll fall off a horse, or slip on wet pavement? So that you don't need to get your hands dirty?" Rose sneered at him.

He smiled his cold smile. "Keeping one's hands clean— maintaining one's innocence. Is that not the human way?"

"What would you know about it?"

"A great deal. After all, I was once human." The king

gestured to his sons, standing in silence around them. "And their mothers were all human, just as your mother was human and you are human. And your children and your sisters' children will be three-parts human." The king laughed. "What joy it will bring me, to know that my grandchildren will be free to walk in the daylight world!"

Rose had thought she was beyond fear, but she had been wrong. At these words a cold thrill of terror went through her and she staggered, near to fainting, imagining her children walking the streets of Westfalin to do the bidding of the King Under Stone. Illiken caught her, steadying her with his hard, cold hands. She shook him off, turning to a sofa for support instead.

"I will not stay here," she said, hating the tremor in her voice. "I will not marry Illiken. I will not have his child. . . . You cannot make me!"

"Oh, but I can," the King Under Stone said in reasonable tones. "In one week's time you will marry Illiken, and never see the sunlight again, dear Rose. Don't you understand that?"

Hope flickered in Rose. "But you have to let us go, that's the contract. We dance, and then we go home, and when the years are up we're free. You're bound by the contract, even as we are."

"Contracts can be broken, if one is willing to pay the price," the king purred. "And what is one life, after all?" He reached out and stroked the cheek of one of his sons, whose eyes widened in terror.

"So." Rose felt nauseated now, as well as faint. "One of your sons will die so that you can keep us here?"

"The penalty for breaking the contract is a life." The king

shrugged. "And I do not intend it to be my own." He pushed the prince away. "Now go to your room and stay there," he ordered Rose, all silk gone from his voice and only the stone beneath remaining.

Rose went.

"Are you all right?" Lily took one look at Rose's face and helped her older sister onto a sofa. "What happened?"

She told them everything, not even sparing the younger set. They had to know. It was their right and their burden, to share among themselves. When she was done, they were all weeping.

"What will we do now?" Violet collapsed rather than sat next to Rose. "We're trapped here forever!"

"Galen's going to die," Rose said softly. "And we're going to marry the princes."

"Except for the one who has to die as punishment," Poppy pointed out. "I hope it's Blathen." Blathen was her partner at the Midnight Ball.

"He'll just have another son," Rose said softly, having truly seen into the king's mind. "With another unfortunate woman. And then you'll be married to a baby."

"Why are there always twelve?" Orchid wanted to know.

"Twelve what?" Lily retied Orchid's sash.

"Twelve of us. And twelve princes. That's so many. . . ."

Rose was piecing it all together in her mind. "There were twelve magicians who imprisoned the king here," she said. "And if we each have one child, there will be twelve part-human, part-witch children for the king to use. He's going to get them to break open his prison, I know it."

They all shivered.

They would never see their father again.

Poor Anne would be hung as a witch and Galen would be killed. And they would be trapped here, year after year, with *him* and his silent, sullen sons.

Tears leaked out of Rose's eyes despite her resolve to stop crying. For the first time she understood what Lily had gone through when her Heinrich died, and felt a stab of sympathy.

"We have to get out of here," Rose announced.

"How?" Jonquil countered, shaking her head. "We can't just walk out the door. Someone will see us."

"We'll wait until the ball," Rose began.

Poppy interrupted her. "There's no way to get across the lake." She shook her head, pleating her dark skirts with nervous fingers. "We're going to have to marry them, sooner rather than later." There was a catch in her voice.

"We have to get the king to let us go back home, even if it's just for a few minutes," Rose said, thinking furiously. "If we could just get back there, we could find a way to stay."

"And how do we convince him to let us go back?" Violet's voice was devoid of hope. "He's got us right where he's always wanted us."

"But not where *he* wants to be," Rose said.

"What?" Lily frowned, and Violet shook her head.

"What are you talking about, Rose? You know that the king cannot go into the daylight world," Violet said.

"Saints be praised," said Hyacinth, and muttered a prayer under her breath.

"But his sons can," Rose reminded them.

The prayer on Hyacinth's lips was choked off. The younger set didn't understand, but the older girls did, and they all stared in silent horror at Rose.

Finally Lily spoke. "What do you mean?" she asked.

Rose said flatly, "The princes can leave at night, so I'll invite them to meet Father. We'll just have to find a way to stay behind when they leave at dawn."

"And what if they find a way to stay above?" Jonquil pointed a shaking finger at Rose. "Have you thought of that?"

"Well, I suppose that would be a risk," Rose admitted. "But it's a risk that we must take, if we want to see Father again. If we want to see the sun again!"

Lily got up and walked over to Rose. She took Rose's hand, gazing intently into her older sister's face. "Are you well, Rose? Do you feel a fever coming on?"

"No," Rose said, pulling away. She looked desperately from Lily to her other sisters. "Don't you see: we have to get out of this! I don't care if I do have to invite them into our home. I'll die before I marry Illiken!"

"I'm with Rose," Violet said staunchly, getting to her feet to stand beside her eldest sister.

"And me," Poppy agreed. "And so is Daisy." She hauled up her twin with her.

"Poppy, it's hardly right to—"

"Oh! I'm sorry: did you *want* to marry Tirolian?" Poppy asked.

Daisy's mouth shut with an audible click.

The younger set stood up as well. "We don't want to marry anyone, ever," Orchid announced for them all.

"But, Rose," Lily protested. "Surely there's a better way than *this*."

"Then I'll give us two days to figure that out," said Rose. "But then, unless anyone has a better idea, I'm inviting Under Stone's sons to take tea with Father."

Warrior

Galen woke with his face stuck to a wooden floor and a terrible throbbing in his head. He thought that a noise had awakened him, but now he couldn't remember what that noise was.

Blearily he blinked and tried to look around, but everything was dark. He panicked for a moment, wondering if the blow had rendered him blind, then realized that it was just . . . dark. Groaning, he tried to sit up, but his hands and feet had been bound.

Squirming until he was at least more comfortable, he knocked his head against a wall, and then his feet, which was when he realized that he was in a wardrobe or some other small space. Now that he had changed position, he could see a faint line of light beneath the door. He pushed against it, but it didn't budge.

His hands were bound in front, which made it quite easy to reach into his right boot and pull out the little knife sheathed there. All his other weapons had been removed, but they apparently hadn't checked his boots. As he reversed the blade and carefully sawed at the rope around his wrists, he shook his head over the laxness.

His bonds parted and he moved to the rope around his ankles, holding the knife awkwardly in his stiff fingers. He'd nicked himself cutting the wrist ropes, and he dropped the knife and had to fumble in the dark for it to get his ankles free, but he eventually succeeded.

Carefully sheathing the knife, Galen staggered to his feet and felt around his prison. It was definitely a wardrobe, locked on the outside. He shouted and kicked at the door and then listened carefully. There was no reply from the room beyond, or even a stirring that he could hear, so it seemed that he was alone.

"Good," he grunted.

Slumping to the floor, he sat against the back of the wardrobe and braced his feet on the door. Drawing his knees in, he kicked out hard and felt it give a little, with a satisfying sound. He kicked again, and a third time, before the door splintered and burst outward, hanging crazily by one hinge. Galen clambered to his feet and stepped out.

He was in Angier's bedchamber, which he'd previously glimpsed through the sitting room door. A chime drew Galen's attention to an ornate wooden clock on the wall. It was just striking half-past midnight. Galen realized that it was the chime that had awakened him, and cursed. Half-past midnight! Rose and her sisters had been trapped below for a full day now.

And Angier was not in bed, sleeping the sleep of the just and holy. Where had he gone?

Galen ran out of the bedroom and into the sitting room beyond. On the table with the books and diary were his weapons and the contents of his satchel.

Galen hastily put the goblet, twigs, handkerchief of sand, and the woolen chain in the satchel, then his powder and shot. He sheathed his knives, checked and holstered his pistols, and fixed his bayonet to his rifle. Then he took up the satchel and the long knife, hung the cape over one shoulder, and headed for the door.

Angier's sitting room had been locked from the outside, but that didn't stop Galen for long. His head still ached, but his thoughts were clear. If he didn't solve this tonight, Rose would die. He broke the lock on the door with one kick and stepped into the hallway.

In the princesses' sitting room, the rug was in place and the maids snored in their chairs. Galen knelt beside the golden maze pattern and put his hand on it. He traced the pattern with a fingertip as he had seen Lily do and said a prayer.

Nothing.

Was he too late, or would it simply not work for him?

He reached into his satchel to take out one of the silver twigs, thinking that the blessed silver might help. As he did so, the handkerchief tumbled out and grains of glittering black sand scattered across the rug. They sparkled in the light from the candles. The golden maze pattern glowed and the fibers fused together into gold bars, but they did not sink into the floor. Galen sprinkled on a little more sand, but it had no effect. He put the handkerchief away and gripped a silver twig in his right hand. Uttering another prayer, he traced the pattern with the gleaming twig.

The sand sparkled even brighter, and the golden lines widened and sank into the floor. The twig itself dissolved, and Galen drew back just in time to avoid falling headfirst down the spiral staircase. He got to his feet and ran down the stairs, reaching the bottom only seconds after the last rung settled into place.

The pearl and silver gate swung open at his touch and he passed into the forest, pausing only to fasten his purple cape. Running down the path, he felt his blood drumming in his ears. *Rose, Rose, Rose,* his pulse seemed to say. *Save her, save her, save her.*

But the lake posed another problem. There was no golden boat in which to ride, no tall prince to row him across. Galen could swim, but it would ruin his rifle and pistols, and he wasn't sure that the black liquid filling the lake was even water. He crouched down and touched a careful finger to it, and his skin began to burn. Galen had to spit on his finger to stop the burning.

"No swimming, then," Galen said aloud.

He pulled out another of the silver twigs, and cast it on the water, praying for a bridge of some sort.

No bridge formed. The twig sank into the black waves and Galen kicked the sand in rage. He started to walk along the

edge of the shore, the black castle always looming in the corner of his eye. To the right, a few of the silver trees had sprung up right at the water's edge. He shoved at one of them, trying to see how securely rooted in the loose sand it was. There was no time to make a raft, though, and the tree didn't budge.

But then he saw what was beyond the tree.

A boat, made of lacy silver filigree, had been pulled up among the trees and beached there. It looked as if it would sink in an instant, but hope fluttered in Galen's breast. He bent and inspected it. It looked like a piece of silver lace, hardened and curved, and there was a scrap of blue satin snagged on one of the oarlocks.

It was well known that blue had been Queen Maude's favorite color; she had worn it in every portrait that Galen had seen.

"So that is how she got across," Galen said under his breath.

Then he grabbed the edge of the boat and hauled it down to the water. He said a silent prayer as it slid onto the black waves, and watched without breathing as it bobbed there. No water seeped in; it floated as lightly as a dry leaf. Not wanting to waste any more time, Galen leaped aboard and grabbed the silver oars. With every stroke his urgency intensified again, and the slap of the water against the lacy hull whispered for him to hurry.

It was even more disconcerting to see the princesses tonight than it had been the three previous nights. They were dressed

in the cobweb-fine silks of the kingdom Under Stone, clinging gowns of purple, ebony, and indigo that looked like bruises to Galen's eyes. Their faces, normally pale and resigned in this place, were filled with despair now, and several of them sobbed openly.

He searched for Rose and found her on the far side of the ballroom, deep in conversation with Illiken as they danced. Eyes narrowed, worried about what she was up to, Galen wound between the figures of the dance until he was near enough to hear her.

"If I made a contract with your father, to allow you to come above for one night, would you promise not to harm any member of my household?"

Galen's breath exploded out in a "No!"

Rose and her suitor both froze. The couples around them for several paces froze as well, and all turned to see who had shouted.

Color bloomed in Rose's cheeks. "What was that sound?" She looked around with an air of obviously feigned inno-cence. "Did you hear that, Illiken?"

"Of course I heard it," he said stiffly. "Something is amiss here." He glared around, his gaze passing over Galen several times, but Illiken's power was not great enough to allow him to see through the cape's influence. He turned to a servant. "Beg my lord father's presence," he commanded.

"Your lord father is already here," said a wintry voice.

The doors at the end of the ballroom had opened sound-lessly while the courtiers' attention had been on Rose.

"What has happened?" The king sat on his throne as if he couldn't care less, but his eyes were fixed on Rose the entire time.

"Forgive me, lord," Jonquil said, curtsying. Of the princesses, she had been the nearest to Rose. "I coughed suddenly, and it disrupted the dance."

"You . . . coughed?" The king raised his eyebrows, clearly not believing a word of Jonquil's excuse. "I see." The pale king's skepticism was palpable. "Rionin?"

Jonquil's suitor snapped to attention. "My lord father?"

"Did she, in fact, cough?"

Confusion clouded the prince's handsome face. "I wasn't paying attention."

The king's gaze wandered over the assembly, and once again his eyes lingered on the spot where Galen stood.

Illiken, of all people, came to the rescue.

"My lord father, may I speak with you?"

The king nodded, then waved to the musicians' gallery for them to continue. The dancing started up again, with the exception of Rose, who went to the chairs along the wall to sit down, and Illiken, who bent one knee to speak low words to his father.

"What are you plotting?" Galen hissed to Rose.

She didn't even jump at the sound of his disembodied voice. "I had to try *something*."

"Inviting Under Stone's son aboveground? What earthly good could that do?"

"I wanted a chance to go home again," she hissed. "I thought we could elude them, once we were there."

"Just like your mother wanted children, and an end to the

war?" The words were harsh, but Galen didn't regret them. It was madness to even think about striking another bargain with the King Under Stone.

"I didn't know what else to do," Rose said, her voice sounding choked.

"I do." Galen squeezed her elbow. "Slip along the wall here, and leave. There's a silver boat between the island and the shore. Get out of here."

"A boat? What boat? And what about my sisters?"

"We'll get them. They won't all fit. I'll have to make two trips, so hurry."

Lily interrupted him. "Rose! What have you done?" She pointed to the dais, where her suitor and Jonquil's had joined Illiken and their father in an intense conversation. The king was watching them, however, his eyes on Rose.

"I asked Illiken some questions," Rose said. "But I am not going to invite them above after all."

"Nice that you've come to your senses," the normally sweet-natured Lily snapped.

"Lily," Rose said gently. "Slip out of the room, go to the lake, and wait by the silver boat there."

"What?" Lily stared at her sister.

"Take Petunia and Pansy with you," Rose went on. "Say you're taking them to freshen up." Her eyes flickered, unseeing, in Galen's direction. "I need to stay and help the others," she said.

"I'll do that," he insisted.

Lily started at the sound of his voice. "What was that? Galen?" She had the sense to whisper.

He put a hand on her wrist, just lightly, and she shivered. "I'm right here, Your Highness. I've found a boat—I think it was your mother's. It won't hold you all at once, so we must hurry."

"But we'll anger the king—"

"You'll be out of his reach, forever," Galen assured her with confidence he did not entirely feel. He glanced up at the dais, and saw the princes looking their way, along with their father. "Go, now! Hurry!"

Lily straightened her shoulders and tossed her head. "Well, Rose," she said in a carrying voice. "I'll do it myself, then."

She marched onto the dance floor and tapped Pansy's prince on the shoulder. "Excuse me." Lily was speaking in a normal tone now and Galen could just barely make out the words. "I think that the younger set had better visit the retiring room. They've had quite a lot of excitement tonight." She took Pansy's hand and led her from her bemused partner.

Petunia's prince had apparently heard the exchange, because he stepped away with a small bow as Lily sailed over to him. She had to interrupt Orchid and her partner, though. Orchid's prince was busy watching the dais, and as soon as he distractedly handed Orchid to Lily, he went over and bowed to his father, a question on his lips.

"Hurry, hurry," Galen muttered in a low voice. He saw Iris ask Lily something when they passed her, and join the string of princesses with an expression of relief on her face. "They're drawing too much attention now," he muttered, seeing the pale king shift his attention from Rose to Lily and the four younger girls. "Too many at once."

"They'll be fine," Rose said out of the corner of her mouth. "Just don't panic."

"Rose!" The King Under Stone's voice cut through the music. "Join us, won't you?"

Black Wool Chain

Don't do it," Galen said as Rose walked toward the dais.

"I have to," she whispered. "It will distract him." She wound her way between the remaining dancers, most of whom were too busy watching the king and the princes to do much more than sway in place.

Galen followed on her heels, only peripherally aware that the other princesses had stopped dancing and were also moving toward the dais. He saw Poppy whisper something to Jonquil, who nodded. "Go, Poppy. Go, Jonquil. Run while you can," Galen thought. He knew that he should follow them, to row the boat across and back for Rose, but he couldn't leave her side.

"Dear Rose," the King Under Stone said when they reached the dais. "What is this you were asking Illiken about? You wish my sons to visit the mortal realm?"

"It was a passing thought," Rose said airily, but Galen was standing close enough to see her trembling. "I thought my father should meet them, sire, before we all wed. But it seems that they cannot all leave at once, so perhaps it is not important after all."

"Not important?" The pale king raised his eyebrows. "To assure your father that his precious girls will be in good hands?" The king rubbed his hands together as if to illustrate, and the dry sound they made gave Galen chills.

Galen saw Poppy, Daisy, and Jonquil moving toward the doors of the ballroom. Rose had a fine dew of sweat on her forehead and was trembling harder than ever. Worrying about how to get her out of the ballroom, he felt cautiously in his satchel with his left hand until he found a particular silver twig.

One he had etched a name on, earlier that day.

"Pardon me, sire," Violet said, coming to stand near Rose. Galen moved out of her way just before she ran into him. She had an arm around Hyacinth, and Lilac trailed behind them.

"What is it, dear Violet?"

"We only wondered if Rose was feeling well," Violet said. "She looked flushed." She put up her chin and bravely faced the king. "Hyacinth is not at her best, either, and I wondered if we might retire to our chambers soon."

Hyacinth said nothing. She did lean closer to Violet, though, resting her head on the other's shoulder. Lilac nodded and took Hyacinth's free hand. Galen groaned silently, wishing they had just left without attracting the king's notice.

"Now, my dears, surely you would not deny me the pleasure of watching you dance—" The king's eyes narrowed, and

he looked beyond the four princesses before him. "Where are the others?"

If Galen had found the King Under Stone's appearance unsettling before, it was nothing compared to how he looked now. White face so pale with rage that it appeared carved from bone, the king seemed to grow ever taller, head and shoulders above even his sons.

"*Now*, Rose!" Galen shouted. He grabbed her arm and shoved her toward the door.

"You! Where are you?" the pale king screamed, searching for the source of Galen's voice. "I can almost see you!"

Galen steeled himself for what he had to do, and then he cast his doubts away and acted.

Switching the silver twig to his right hand, he leaped onto the dais and stabbed the King Under Stone in the chest. Galen kept his hand locked around the shaft of the twig until he forced the immortal ruler back into the black throne.

A roar filled the air, and winds buffeted Galen. He held to the silver twig even tighter, not knowing what would happen if he let go. Ghostly hands seemed to squeeze Galen's heart, his lungs, his skull, and he thought for a moment that he would die as the ancient magicians had died. But Under Stone was weaker now, and rather than exploding out to wreak havoc on the world, as the magicians had feared, his powers ebbed away into the vessel that waited at his side.

Illiken.

Illiken staggered, and the color leeched from his skin and hair. Galen let go of the silver needle piercing Under Stone's

heart, and reached for a pistol with shaking hands as the room exploded with screams.

The courtiers saw their king shudder and then slump against the back of his throne. Their screams were almost drowned out by Illiken's howls as his father's powers transformed him. Several of the other princes rushed onto the dais, their faces rigid with horror.

Galen glanced around quickly, and saw with relief that Rose and the last three princesses had slipped away during the commotion.

Unfortunately, Illiken saw the same thing.

"Rose!" Illiken shouted. "My bride, my brothers' brides! They are escaping! Get them!"

The guards surged out the doors of the ballroom, with Under Stone's hideous court following them. Galen jumped off the dais and pushed his way into the crowd, trying to get to the front, to reach the shore before . . .

He slowed for just a second, and then fought his way out of the rush with renewed anxiety. How to get all twelve princesses across the lake in one boat? Would Lily have been able to row the younger set across herself? He could only hope.

He was the first one out of the doors and onto the beach, but only by a few seconds. And there, to his horror, he saw the twelve princesses standing on the shore looking lost.

The princes' twelve boats were too far down the shore. The silver boat, when at last he located it, was out in the middle of the lake, drifting aimlessly. In his haste to reach Rose, he had

not pulled it far enough up the shore. He cursed his own stupidity, then called out to Rose.

She looked around blindly, and he realized that he still wore the cape. He snatched it over his head and tucked it under one arm as he ran. The other princesses cried out to see him appear so suddenly.

Their pursuers were pounding down the beach, Illiken in the lead. Rose pulled her shawl closer about her shoulders, looking around for another way to cross.

"White like a swan, floating on the water," Galen said, staring at her shawl and wondering. . . .

Rose looked at him, not understanding. He grabbed a corner of the shawl. "The wool, Rose, a magician gave it to me. . . ."

Before he could finish the thought, Rose had nodded and taken it off. Galen cast it on the water.

Before their eyes, the wool stiffened and stretched until it became a triangular raft large enough to hold them all. Galen sagged for a moment in relief, then he scooped up Pansy and Petunia and jumped onto the white raft, the others following suit. As soon as Hyacinth, the last, boarded, the enchanted craft began to speed across the lake.

"They're coming!" Poppy pointed behind them to where the princes were launching the golden boats with inhuman speed.

"Do you know how to load a pistol?" Galen looked to Rose, but it was Lily who answered.

"I do," she said, taking the pistols out of his hands. "A friend taught me." She loaded the pistols with expert skill while Galen attended to his rifle.

"Hold them ready," he told Lily. "Can you shoot?"

She nodded, and Galen remembered that it was Lily who had threatened Rionin and the others when they had come into the garden.

They reached the far shore and ran onto the black sand. Instantly the white shawl shrank and then disappeared beneath the water.

"Get the others home," Galen told Rose. He stood on the shore, his rifle ready. "Wait until you have a good shot," he instructed Lily, who stood by his side looking pale but calm. "Don't waste it. There isn't enough time to reload."

"I understand," she said. She steadied the pistol in both hands.

"Now for the rifle," he said, as the front boat came within range. He aimed for Illiken, but the new king lunged to the side as Galen squeezed the trigger. The sound of the shot rang through the underworld, and another prince who had shared Illiken's boat cried out and gripped his arm.

Galen shouldered the rifle and raised his pistol. Beside him, Lily took careful aim. Galen looked for Illiken once more, but he was crouched low in his boat now, and Galen could not get a clear shot. Instead he aimed for the second boat and fired. The prince guiding that boat fell back, his boat rocking wildly, and the guard with him cried out as they tipped into the lake.

"Ha!" Lily cried out as she fired, and the prince she had been aiming for clutched his shoulder and fell back into the arms of one of his brothers. "Swine," she screamed, her face flushed.

Galen looked at her and saw tears on her cheeks. "He was my partner," she explained.

"Run," he replied, taking her hand. Illiken's boat was scraping the sand in the shallows.

They raced for the forest, where they found Rose waiting. "I told you to go," he huffed as they passed into the silvery shadows of the trees.

"I know," Rose said, falling in beside him. "But I couldn't leave you! And how will we stop Illiken? He's king now, *and* half human. He can cross into the mortal world in the darkness."

"Isn't it dawn yet?" Lily's flush was fading to pallor again.

"I don't think so," Rose panted.

"Not for two more hours at least," Galen told them.

They could see the others up ahead, just reaching the pearl and silver gate. Behind them came the crunching of booted feet on the path and the sound of shouts, like the baying of hunting hounds. There was crashing in the trees to their left: a fast runner braving the silver trees to head them off.

Galen whipped his musket off his shoulder and veered toward the sound. With a shout he thrust the bayonet forward, cutting off the triumphant cry of one of the princes as he broke out of the trees.

The bayonet stuck fast, and Galen left it to continue on. Holding his arms wide, he swept Rose and Lily before him through the gate. The other princesses waited at the foot of the golden stairs.

Illiken stopped his headlong run to step casually through

the gate and smile at them. "Come to me, Rose." He held out one hand, imperious.

Rose swayed beside Galen. Galen put out an arm and stopped her.

"Our mother's bargain ends with your father's death," Rose said bravely, although her face was strained with the effort of resisting him.

"The bargain passes to me, even as it passed from your mother to you," Illiken said with a sneer. "Now, come!"

Some of the princesses had ascended the steps, but others had lingered, to Galen's mounting anxiety. A soft hand touched his wrist, and from behind him Lily whispered, "Here." A pistol was pressed into his hand.

Galen took it, holding it down and slightly behind him. He edged a little away from Rose, so that he could bring the weapon up swiftly.

"Come now, Rose," Illiken repeated. "Perhaps your punishment for trying to flee should be that you and I wed now, tonight."

Galen brought the pistol up in a smooth movement and fired. The ball struck true, hitting Illiken square in the heart and throwing him back against the gate. He slumped to the ground, and Galen nudged Rose toward the golden stair. He had one last thing to do before he left.

Illiken groaned and got to his feet like a marionette being pulled upright. "A good effort, gardener," he said, brushing off his jacket. "But mere iron can no longer slay me, for I am the King Under Stone now!" He raised his arms, smiling.

"We need another silver needle," Rose whispered. She had put one foot on the bottom step, but now moved back. "Lily," she said to her sister. "Take the others and go. Galen and I will stay to—" And without finishing her sentence, she lunged past Galen, running with her skirts high, past the startled Illiken and into the silver wood.

"No!" Illiken snarled as Rose grabbed the lowest branch of the first tree, dragging on it to break free a twig. He went after her, seizing her by the waist and hauling her down the path toward the lake.

The clasp of the invisibility cloak was still fastened. Galen pulled it on and disappeared, hurrying off the path and into the trees. He reached up and snapped off a twig, then another, as he followed Illiken and Rose.

When they reached the end of the forest, the remaining princes and courtiers met them, helping Illiken hustle Rose toward the waiting boats. Rose broke free, pushing aside the courtiers and running back toward the trees. Galen met her halfway, pulling her into his arms and covering her with the cloak as well. The court of the underworld gasped as the princess vanished.

"I can see you, gardener," Illiken shouted. He came striding up the beach. Like his father, he was squinting at a spot near where Galen and Rose stood, as though he knew they were there but couldn't quite make them out.

"What will we do?" Rose whispered.

"Wait," he whispered back. Galen could feel her heart pounding against his chest. He dropped his arm from her

waist, pulled a knife from his belt, and scratched blindly at the side of the silver twig.

"Aha!" Illiken reached out, his arms wide, as though to embrace them both, still squinting.

Galen's right arm snapped up, and he pierced Illiken through the heart with the twig, on which he had just scrawled the prince's name. Not waiting to see if it worked, Galen wheeled around, keeping Rose under the shelter of his left arm, and ran with her back into the trees. They kept to the shadows, avoiding the path where pale-faced guards searched for them.

"They daren't spend too much time among the trees," Rose whispered as they approached the gate.

They huddled under the spreading branches of the tree nearest the gate. One of the princes stood between them and freedom. With one hand, Galen fished in his satchel for the chain.

"When he looks the other way, run for the gate," he told Rose, who nodded.

Galen tossed a bullet out into the path. The prince jerked and went to get a better look at it. Rose burst out of Galen's arms and flew through the gate, with Galen hard on her heels. The prince turned, shouting, as Galen clanged the gate shut.

"I am the King Under Stone now," the gaunt figure hissed, grabbing the latch from his side. "You cannot stop me!" The color faded from his hair as he spoke.

Galen didn't answer. Steadily he passed one end of the black wool chain through the bars and around the back of the gatepost.

The new king drew back with a cry. "What is that? How have you ...?" He winced and blinked as though the dull black wool burned his eyes.

Still not speaking, Galen wrapped the chain twice more, then slipped one link through another and cinched it tight. From his satchel Galen pulled the final piece of his plan: his mother's little silver crucifix. He jabbed it into the woolen knot. The silver flared bright and the chain turned from wool to steel.

"There," Galen said, feeling a rush of fierce joy as the new King Under Stone drew back with a scream of rage. "That will hold."

Taking Rose by the arm, Galen led her up the golden stairs to the princesses' sitting room. Her sisters were all in a circle around the rug, faces gray with fright. They shrieked with joy to see Galen and Rose emerge, running to embrace the two and kiss their cheeks.

Pansy flung herself into Galen's arms and sobbed into his neck. "I knew you'd save us."

"It's all over now, don't you worry," Galen said, stroking Pansy's hair. Over her head, he saw Daisy watching with a disapproving eye. He winked at her, and she blinked. His arms shaking from exhaustion, he put Pansy down, but she clung to his hand.

"We'll only have to go back tomorrow night," Hyacinth said in a hollow voice.

"No, we won't," Rose told her. "Galen chained the gate shut. We're never going back, and no one can come after us."

The princesses cheered, all except for Hyacinth. She fetched an oil lamp and threw it on the maze-patterned rug without warning. The silk burst into flame, making the other girls shriek and jump out of the way. Galen rushed into one of the bedrooms and grabbed a heavy blanket from one of the beds to smother the fire, but he waited until the rug had been thoroughly burned before tossing down the blanket and stamping on it.

"Very clever, Your Highness," Galen said to Hyacinth once the fire was out.

"You may call me Hyacinth," she said, giving him a tremulous smile. She stepped forward and laid a timid hand on his arm.

Galen smiled back, bent, and kissed her thin cheek. Then, for good measure, he turned and kissed Rose.

On the lips.

Truth

As Rose looked around, blushing and wishing that she hadn't had her first kiss in front of all her sisters (nice as it was), she saw something that startled her. Maria, their maid, was sitting up in her chair and staring at them.

It was not yet dawn.

"Your Highnesses have returned!" Maria shrieked. She clasped her hands to her bosom and began to cry.

"Maria, you're awake!" Rose took a step toward the woman but still clung to Galen's hand. To Rose this seemed even more miraculous than their delivery from the kingdom Under Stone.

Maria frowned around the room through her tears. "Well, the other maids and I waited here in case you returned. I can't believe I slept at all, with all the fuss these past few days." She gave the charred remains of the rug an odd look. "What have my ladies been doing, if I may ask?"

Rose took a deep breath. Here was the first test, to see if the underworld's power over them was truly broken. "We were the prisoners of the King Under Stone," Rose said, quite clearly.

Maria gasped in shock. So did Rose's sisters.

"Rose! You told!" Petunia danced up and down.

"You can say it! We can say it!" Jonquil clapped her hands to her cheeks.

"God be praised," said Hyacinth, and sank to her knees. She began to pray.

Maria crossed herself. "So Master Werner was right." She nodded at Galen. "The king has been in a taking since you shouted out that name in the council this morning, Master Werner, but I don't know if anyone other than myself and two or three maids believed you."

Releasing Galen's hand, Rose crossed to her faithful maid and hugged the woman. "Oh, Maria, it's been simply awful. But it's all over now." She turned back to the others. "We must go to Father at once!"

In the hallway outside their rooms, Rose found Walter Vogel sitting on a chair, an ancient musket in his hands. He got to his feet and bowed stiffly to them. Two guards lay nearby, one with a swollen nose and the other with a bruised jaw.

"Walter! What are you doing here?" Rose put a hand to her throat, startled.

"Funny thing, that," Walter said calmly. "I was sitting at home, smoking my pipe, when there was a knock at the door. An old woman of my acquaintance had come to tell me to get out my musket and bring it to the palace. 'The princesses need guarding,' she told me. 'You keep folks out of their rooms so that Galen can do his job.'" Walter shrugged. "And I did."

"I could have used some help down there," Galen said.

"I'm an old, old man, Galen," Walter said quietly. "Which I think you know. If I'd gone down with you, it would have finished me, and there are still things I must do. Under Stone was not the only one of his kind." The wrinkled face broke into a grin. "And it seems that you did admirably on your own."

"Yes, he did," Rose agreed.

"That bishop's with your father in the council chamber now," Walter warned.

"Good," Rose said. "Walter, I want plenty of witnesses. Will you please come with us?"

"Of course, Your Highness."

Rose led the procession down the hall to the council chamber and entered without knocking. Inside King Gregor sat, not in his usual tall carved chair, but in a smaller chair in the middle of the room. The normally gruff king seemed pale and cowed.

The king's customary chair was occupied by Bishop Angier, who presided over the room with obvious satisfaction. The prime minister and a half dozen of their father's chief councillors were also in attendance, looking variously mutinous or humble, as though they had all been chastised by the bishop.

But even Angier looked stunned by the sudden entrance of Rose, her sisters, Galen, Maria, and Walter. Rose found their shock quite enjoyable, and stood there for a moment to let them all get a good look. She knew that she and her sisters looked awful: their strange dark gowns torn and muddied with sparkling black dirt, faces smudged and sweaty, hair in disarray. Galen had gunpowder stains on his cheek, and Lily's hands were black with it.

"Father," Rose said finally, after everyone had stared enough and she could see Angier starting to swell up prior to making a declaration. She curtsied. Her sisters and maid followed suit; Galen and Walter bowed. "We have returned."

"Returned? From dancing with the devil?" Angier's voice had lost some of its force.

Rose didn't take her eyes off her father, though. "We have long been under a curse, Father," she said. "But it is broken now."

King Gregor looked anxiously at Rose, and then beyond her at his other daughters. "It's over?"

"It's over," Rose told him firmly. She took Galen's arm and drew him forward. "Thanks to Master Werner."

Relief washed over King Gregor's face. The councillors began babbling all at once, and Angier got to his feet, pounding a meaty fist on the arm of his chair and shouting for silence.

"I will conduct this inquiry," the bishop insisted.

"What inquiry?" King Gregor's voice cut through the noisy room. "My daughters have come with joyous news for me. There is no need for an inquiry." He sat up straight and smoothed his coat, his gray, worried complexion clearing minute by minute. "Master Werner, were your words this morning true? Have you at last discovered where my daughters go at night?"

"This is nonsense! These girls have learned the ways of the devil from that Bretoner woman," Angier ranted. "You are fortunate, Gregor, that your station protects you and your daughters—"

"Now, Brother Angier, let us not be too quick to condemn," said a soft voice. In the far corner of the room, as though cast aside by his more flamboyant brother in the church, Bishop Schelker stood. That good man, who had baptized Rose and all her sisters, smiled with relief at the princesses as he came forward.

"Bishop Angier, I confess myself a bit disturbed by the cavalier way in which you seem to have declared King Gregor and his young daughters guilty." His mild blue eyes fixed on Angier, who began to turn very red.

"The archbishop has full confidence in my judgment!" Angier roared.

"Does he?" Schelker pulled a scroll from his sleeve. "I have a letter here from His Holiness, Angier. It arrived just moments ago. He asks how our *joint* investigation of this matter is proceeding. His Holiness also makes reference to the instructions that you were to deliver to me, which I never received."

Angier swallowed and then straightened his cuffs. "Well, Schelker—"

Bishop Schelker interrupted him. "It seems that the archbishop has long been concerned with your overzealous methods in investigating matters of witchcraft, and that you were not his first choice to take care of this matter. But his first choice, and his second, were both quite suddenly indisposed. This

naturally has made His Holiness suspicious. In addition to making certain that King Gregor and his daughters are treated with all respect, he asks me to keep an eye on you and to put a halt to matters if I think you have overstepped your bounds. And I believe that you have." Schelker never raised his voice. "Guards. Please escort His Excellency to his rooms, and make sure he stays there. Father Michel, too."

Angier adjusted his robes with great dignity and swept out before the guards could lay a hand on him. As he passed Rose and her sisters, he gave them a vicious look. "Evil never triumphs," he hissed at them.

"I know," Rose retorted.

The guards did have to lead away a babbling, wild-eyed Father Michel, who was insisting that he knew nothing of the other bishops' illnesses, and that he was an innocent man. Schelker watched with a look of deep disappointment, then turned back to King Gregor and gave a little nod.

King Gregor, in turn, looked to Galen. "Now that that unpleasantness is done, would you please enlighten us all?" His normal brusque manner was back.

Galen came forward and bowed again amid the babble that arose from the council. He held up a hand for silence, waited until he got it, then said, "Your Majesty, every night, a deep sleep would fall upon your daughters' attendants. The princesses then descended a golden stair through the floor of their sitting room." He pulled something from the pouch at his belt: a charred bit of silk. "This was the rug that transformed into the staircase, now destroyed by fire at the hands of Princess Hyacinth." He laid it on the table in front of King Gregor.

"They passed through a gate of silver and pearl and into a forest of silver trees." Galen reached over and plucked something from Rose's hair. She started and he smiled at her, then laid a silver leaf before her father.

King Gregor lifted the silver leaf and studied it carefully. All along the table, the councillors watched Galen with rapt attention.

"After the forest they were met on the shores of a great black lake by twelve suitors, who took them in golden boats to a palace on an island at the center of the lake." Galen took out a handkerchief and spread it before the king, revealing the remaining teaspoonful of glittering black sand. "There they danced till dawn with their suitors, the sons of the King Under Stone." And Galen produced a silver goblet set with precious stones. "It was he who held your daughters in thrall. He who kept them from speaking a word of this enchantment."

The prime minister could not hold back. "And how was it that this fiend got control of the princesses? Young ladies of their upbringing do not have dealing with devils!"

"Nor did they." Galen addressed him calmly. Rose had started forward, a protest on her lips, but Galen squeezed her hand and stopped her. "At least, not of their own will.

"They were bound by the ill-made promise of another," Galen said. "They are innocent of witchcraft, as is their father.

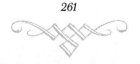

The deaths of those princes were brought about by the King Under Stone, who was as real as you or I, and as evil as Bishop Schelker is good. The King Under Stone did this without the knowledge or the aid of the princesses. But now he is dead, many of his sons are dead, and those that live are bound within their dark realm."

"How can you be sure?" King Gregor put a protective hand on Hyacinth's arm.

"Galen made a chain," Rose said, stepping forward. After years of enforced silence, she couldn't bear to let Galen be the one to tell the whole story. "Of black wool knit with silver needles made from the branches of this tree." She held up the leaf. "The trees in the underworld were sprouted by Mama's brooch, the one given to her by her godfather in Breton. The gate is chained, and the knot pierced with a silver cross. The creatures of the Kingdom Under Stone can no longer influence our world."

"You did this?" King Gregor was on his feet now, looking at Galen like a man reprieved. "You saved my daughters and barred the underworld?"

"Yes, sire," Galen said quietly. "Walter Vogel helped me, and so did Fraulein Anne. I had the cook boil the chain with basil and nightshade, to strengthen it, and the cross was my mother's."

"He was invisible!" Petunia could no longer be contained either. "He was running around, and shooting the bad princes, and yelling, and he threw me and Pansy on the raft so that we could get away. Oh! The shawl he made Rosie was magic, and

it turned into a raft! And he gave Lily a gun, and she shot someone!"

Pansy tugged her father's sleeve. "And he made me this," she whispered, and showed King Gregor her now rather mangled red puff ball.

"Did he?" King Gregor lifted Pansy in his arms. "What a brave young man!" He gave Galen a speculative look. "And how exactly were you able to make yourself invisible, Master Werner?"

"With this," Galen said. He drew a dull purple cape from his satchel and threw it about his shoulders. When he fastened the gold clasp, he disappeared.

Even having seen it before, several of Rose's sisters cried out, along with the councillors. Petunia clapped, though, and stepped forward to poke the air where he had been.

"Galen, where are you?"

"Right here."

Petunia was lifted in the air by invisible hands. Then she disappeared too. They both reappeared a moment later, and Galen put her down, looking exhausted but smiling all the same.

"I went under the cape and went invisible," Petunia squealed. "Rosie! Did you see?"

"I saw," Rose said, taking her hand. Her gaze was on Bishop Schelker.

But it was the prime minister who spoke.

"So," Lord Schiller said. "Witchcraft!"

"Oh, stuff!" The minister of finance, an elderly man with thin wisps of white hair, spoke up. "Such magical artifacts

were common in my grandmother's day. I remember her telling me of seven league boots and the like." He held out a tremulous hand. "May I see that cape?"

"Of course, sir." Galen handed it over, but with reluctance. "It was given to me by an old woman I met on my way here to Bruch," he said.

"A witch," someone hissed.

"I believe she may have been one of the magicians who bound Under Stone into his prison," Galen said, stopping all further comment. Even Bishop Schelker merely nodded and looked thoughtful.

"Whoever she was, if she ever comes to my gate I shall make her a baroness," Rose's father said. He turned to address his councillors. "Are you yet satisfied that my daughters are not guilty of the deaths of those unfortunate princes?"

The councillors argued, they muttered and pounded the table. Walter remained silent, and when Galen looked to him, the old man simply shrugged. There was no way, Galen supposed, that Walter could prove who he was.

Bishop Schelker asked that Angier's accusations be discounted, since he had overstepped his authority. As for himself, the quiet Westfalian bishop clearly believed that Galen and the princesses were innocent of any wrongdoing.

King Gregor finally shouted, "Enough! *I* am the king, and if I am satisfied, then you all are too!" The councillors closed their mouths and subsided.

King Gregor studied Galen for a moment. "Young man, I know that you offered your aid without anticipation of reward,

and for that I commend you." The councillors all banged their fists on the table in agreement. "But in light of the great service you have rendered my daughters, and your country, I believe that some reward is in order." More banging.

Galen was bright red to the tips of his ears. "Really, sire, I had no thought but to save Ro— to help the princesses."

Rose felt her own blush burning up her cheeks. She doubted that anyone had missed Galen's slip of the tongue, and thought that her heart would beat its way right out of her chest with joy.

Her father's lips twitched in amusement. "I think it would be unfair of me not to reward the man who saved my girls, and my kingdom. And it would be more than unfair to offer a lesser reward, simply because your nobleness of spirit is not matched by a noble name.

"Galen Werner, you may choose one of my daughters to be your bride, and when I die you shall sit beside her as co-ruler of Westfalin."

"Your Majesty, I—"

"Take it, boy!" shouted the minister of finance.

"You deserve it, Galen," Walter said with great conviction.

"You do, indeed," Bishop Schelker said. He shot Walter a shrewd look.

"I—I don't know—"

Rose felt her knees shaking. Did he not love her after all?

"Psst, Galen?" Pansy tugged on his arm. Galen leaned down. "If Rose doesn't want you," the little girl whispered loudly, "you can marry me."

Galen laughed shakily. "Thanks, Pansy."

"Oh, Rose! Don't just stand there like a lump," Poppy said, poking her in the back. "If he's too embarrassed, *you* should be the one to say something."

"Poppy!" Daisy looked scandalized. "It's not Rose's place to—"

Under cover of their squabbling, Rose took Galen's hand and moved closer to him. "Do you want to marry me?" she whispered in a much quieter tone than Pansy had.

"Yes," he said.

"If neither of you is going to speak up," King Gregor said, "I shall simply decide it myself!"

"Father," Rose protested, "that won't be necessary!"

"I choose Rose," Galen blurted out at the same time.

"There. Done. Easy." King Gregor clapped his hands. "Now, I believe a feast is in order. Someone send to the kitchens for some food and drink."

"Yes, sir," Rose and Galen said in unison, both of them grinning broadly.

Spring

Galen married Rose under a canopy of white silk, erected by the swan fountain where they had first met. Thanks to the hard work of Reiner, Walter, and the rest of the gardeners, the Queen's Garden had never looked lovelier.

At Galen's suggestion, the ancient oak tree where he suspected Maude and the dark princes crossed between the mortal world and the realm of Under Stone was torn out. The ground was blessed by Bishop Schelker, and a rowan tree was planted instead.

Galen had offered to help, but the king had knighted him, and it wouldn't have been proper. Walter had made each princess a crown out of the flowers she was named for. Rose was resplendent in her white gown with white and red roses encircling her brow.

Bishop Schelker performed the service. He had successfully petitioned to have the Interdict lifted and the rites of the church restored to Westfalin. Angier and Father Michel had been escorted back to Roma in disgrace.

The details behind the princesses' mystery had not been revealed to the public, but the archbishop had issued a public statement declaring the deaths of the princes accidental and pardoning the royal family and Anne.

At the insistence of the princesses, there was no dancing at the wedding reception. Instead, sofas had been positioned all around the garden so that people could sit to talk and eat. Galen saw Walter taking advantage of a pink-upholstered sofa beneath a spreading elm tree and raised his glass. Walter raised his own glass in return, and so did his companion. Galen blinked: he hadn't noticed before, but an elderly woman in a dull purple gown was seated beside Walter. Around her waist was a bulky blue sash that looked as if it had started out life as a woolen scarf. Galen blinked again, and Walter and the woman were gone.

"Rose, did you see—"

But Galen never did finish his question. A young man in a worn soldier's uniform was limping up the path from the rear of the gardens. As he passed each group of revelers, they fell silent and watched him. Looking down, Galen could see that Rose was staring at the young man, her face pale.

"Lily," Rose said in a choked voice. "Lily!"

Lily, who had been wiping cake off Petunia's face, turned around. She saw the young man and dropped her damp handkerchief. He broke into as much of a run as he could manage, and Lily fairly flew into his arms.

"Heinrich," she sobbed.

"Heinrich!" Galen's cousin Ulrike screamed with joy and ran to the young man, hovering impatiently until he finished kissing Lily and could embrace her as well.

Tante Liesel fainted, and the widow Zelda Weiss rushed to her side. Galen started to go to her as well, but Rose held him back, her eyes wide as she nodded toward Reiner Orm.

Reiner's face was dark. "Ulrike," he barked. "Get away from that man!"

"But it's Heinrich," Ulrike said through her tears.

Now she and Lily were holding hands with Heinrich, the three of them standing in a circle. With a shaking finger, Lily traced the long white scar that ran down one side of Heinrich's face. He raised her hand and kissed it.

"My son," Liesel moaned as Zelda revived her.

"Mother." Limping painfully, Heinrich started toward her, one arm still around Lily.

"We have no son," Reiner said.

"That is a shame," King Gregor said. "Because it seems to me that my daughter Lily is quite fond of that young man. And with her eldest sister married, I am looking for a suitable match for Lily."

Rose chimed in, "Soldiers make very good husbands, Father." She put her arm around Galen's waist.

"So I am finding, my dear," King Gregor said.

"Sire," Heinrich said, clearly torn between going to his mother and dealing with his father's disownment. "I am Heinrich Orm."

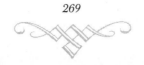

"I know who you are, lad," King Gregor said kindly. The wedding had put him in an expansive mood.

"I love your daughter Lily very much, sire," Heinrich said. Lily, holding tight to his hand, blushed. "Only this injury has kept me from coming to you sooner, to ask for her hand in marriage."

"Oh, Father, please say yes," Lily pleaded, her cheeks wet with tears and her eyes like stars.

"I was with the Eagle Regiment," Heinrich said with pride. "We were the first into Analousia and the last to leave. I was injured while escorting our new ambassador to his first meeting with the Analousian king."

"Is that so?" King Gregor looked impressed.

"He abandoned his duties to the Queen's Garden, sire," Reiner said, his face purple. "He defied my wishes! I have disowned him!"

"Reiner, hold your tongue!" On her feet once more, Tante Liesel came forward and embraced her son, kissing his cheeks and wetting them with her own tears. "I let you place the mourning garland above our door. I let you speak of our son as dead because when word came from the neighbors' sons of the horrors of their first battle, and no letter from Heinrich, I assumed that he *was* dead.

"But he isn't," she went on, her throat choked with more tears. "He's alive! And in love still with his beautiful princess! Can't you see, Reiner? We have been blessed!" She held out a hand to Galen, who took it, Rose still clasped to his other side.

"Our son returned to us! Dear Renata's boy returned and saved the princesses from who knows what horrors! It's a miracle!"

The whole party held their breath, their eyes on Reiner Orm. At last, a suspicious moisture in his eyes, Reiner blew out his breath and nodded his head. "Welcome home, son," he said grudgingly.

"Thank you, sir," Heinrich said.

Reiner reached out as though to shake hands in a manly fashion. Heinrich let go of Lily and his mother and embraced his father.

King Gregor shook his head and muttered something about "stubborn old fool." Galen caught Rose's eye, and they shared a small smile. Then, while Lily helped Heinrich to a sofa and Orchid brought them cake and lemonade, Rose sat down on another sofa with a sigh.

Galen sank down beside her. "So that's my cousin," he said musingly.

"Yes, and that's the great scandal of Bruch as well," Rose said. "The gardener's son fell in love with a princess, and then his father declared him dead when he joined the army." She shook her head. "It was all the gossips could talk about, until our worn-out dancing slippers came to light."

Galen touched her cheek. "Will you never dance with me? I rather enjoyed that time, at the Midnight Ball. But I wouldn't mind being visible, so that you'll step on my toes less often."

Rose made a face at him. "Ha! I'm a wonderful dancer!

But I did promise my father no more worn-out dancing slippers."

"Very well, then," Galen said. He leaned down and pulled off her shoes, tossing them over his shoulder into a lilac bush. "If I may have this dance?" Galen led Rose out onto the smooth lawn and waltzed her across the soft green ground until the sunlight died and stars sparkled in the black night sky.

The Knitting Patterns

A man who knits? Unheard of!

Well, perhaps not . . .

For centuries, commercial knitting guilds were for men only, because knitting was considered too complicated for women! But even after women were allowed to take part in the "manly art" of knitting, men still continued to knit. In many Scandinavian schools, everyone is taught to knit and has to complete a pair of mittens before they can graduate. I had a friend in college who had a beautiful pair of mittens and matching snowflake-pattern hat that her Swedish husband had made in school. And it really wasn't uncommon for soldiers in the first and second World Wars to knit their own socks, washcloths, and hats.

My grandmother started to teach me to knit when I was thirteen years old, but when she had trouble explaining something to me, my grandfather took over. He started knitting to pass the time on long business trips—taught by his boss, no less—and made beautiful blankets for everyone in the family. After he passed away, I finished his last blanket as a gift for my mother.

Rose's Shawl

Materials:
US #13 circular needle
> *(You may choose to start on straight needles, and switch to the longer circular when shawl becomes too large for the straights.)*

Approximately 430 yards bulky weight yarn.
Tapestry needle to finish ends

Instructions:
Cast on 4 stitches. Fasten a safety pin or split-ring marker to the first stitch, to indicate the right side of the work. All odd-numbered rows will start with this marker on the right. Row 1: Knit 1, knit into the front of the next stitch, don't drop it off the left needle, knit into the back of the stitch, drop it off. Repeat, knit last stitch. You now have 6 stitches. Row 2: Knit 2, knit into the front and back of the next 2 stitches, knit 2. 8 stitches. Row 3: Knit across. Row 4: Knit 3, Yarn Over (loop the yarn over the right needle to add a stitch without knitting), purl 2, YO, knit 3. Repeat rows 3 and 4 until piece is 12 inches long. You can now add flower pattern, available as a PDF at www.jessicadaygeorge.com. If pattern is not desired, continue to work Rows 3 and 4 until shawl measures fingertip to fingertip of wearer. Bind off.

The Black Wool Chain

Materials:
US #10 double-pointed needles (set of 4)
1 skein wool yarn

Instructions:
Cast on 24 stitches, dividing them evenly among three needles (8 per needle). Place marker and join for working in the round, careful not to twist. Knit 4 rounds, bind off and weave in ends. Cast on 24 stitches, *slide previous link onto needles* so that it is hanging from your middle needle, making sure that your working yarn is not entangled in the link. Join and knit 4 rounds, bind off. Cast on 24 stitches, slide your links onto the center needle, making sure that your yarn is not entangled and that only one (not both!) of the links is hanging from the new soon-to-be link. Knit 4 rounds, bind off. Continue in this manner for as many links as you can stand to make.

To felt: Put the chain in a zippered pillowcase, or a regular pillowcase (tie the opening in a knot so that the chain doesn't fall out) and wash it on hot/cold with a towel or two to increase agitation. Wash the chain 2-3 times, until it is felted to your satisfaction. Roll it in a towel to squeeze out excess water, and arrange it on another towel to dry, shaping links to your liking.

In addition to more magical uses, the chain can be used as a belt, scarf, or the strap of a bag. Man-made fibers will not felt, nor will "superwash" wool that has been treated to make it washable. Make sure that your yarn is 100% wool or a blend of wool and other natural fibers such as mohair, angora, or soy. The label will often indicate if the yarn will felt or not.

Pronunciation Guide

The continent of Ionia is roughly based on Europe, and Westfalin is much like early-nineteenth-century Germany. The majority of the names used are real German names, and should be pronounced as such. For example, *j* is pronounced as *y*, and *w* is *v*.

Bruch brook
Galen gay-len
Heinrich hine-rick
Illiken Ill-i-ken
Jutta yuh-tuh
Kathe kay-teh
Liesel lee-zell
Reiner ry-ner
Rionin ry-o-nin
Schelker shel-kur
Tante (aunt) tahn-tuh

Ulrike ull-REE-kuh
Vogel foh-gel
Von Aue fon ow-uh
Walter val-ter
Werner ver-ner
Westfalin VEST-fahl-in
Wolfram vulf-rahm

Acknowledgments

I must admit that this isn't the book I originally wrote for my sister, Jenn, but it's still a good one and still for her. The original book for Jenn may never see the light of day, sadly. But as I was pondering who this book might belong to, I thought of her. She introduced me to fantasy books, chaperoned me at World Fantasy Con, and did countless other things well above and beyond the call of normal sisterly duty.

So here you go, my dear, your very own book!

I would be in a rubber-walled room going "glub, blub, glub" right now if it weren't for some amazing people: my long-suffering husband, my sister/therapist/fashion consultant, and the rest of the family, in-laws and all. You couldn't ask for more wonderful, understanding, and supportive people. They have spread the word about my books, watched my kid while I wrote, traveled all over to see me dramatically read and sign at bookstores, and just been all-around fab.

I am especially grateful for my agent, who talks in a

soothing voice when I call up freaking out, and who didn't say, "*Another* fairy tale retelling?" when I told her about this book, but, "Sounds interesting." (And that's why I love her.) And my editor, who didn't say, "*Knitting patterns?!*" when I told her about this book, but, "Oooh!" (And that's why I love *her*. Also, she sends me chocolate.)

The Boy and Pippin were mostly distractions, but they are both Terribly Cute, and I wouldn't be the same without them.

And finally, I would like to thank the good people of Twizzler, whose Strawberry Twists got me through the original writing of this book. Also, the fine makers of Canada Dry Ginger Ale, who got me through the rewrite when I realized that the sick feeling in my stomach wasn't nerves—it was Baby 2.0!